CHILDREN OF THE DUST

CHILDREN OF THE DUST

LOUISE LAWRENCE

HARPER & ROW, PUBLISHERS

Library of Congress Cataloging in Publication Data
Lawrence, Louise, 1943–
  Children of the dust.

  Summary: After a nuclear war devastates the earth,
a small band of people struggles for survival in a
new world where children are born with mutations.
  [1. Nuclear warfare—Fiction. 2. Survival—
Fiction. 3. Science fiction] I. Title.
PZ7.L4367Ch 1985   [Fic]   85-42618
ISBN 0-06-023738-4
ISBN 0-06-023739-2 (lib. bdg.)

FOR THE CHILDREN

THAT THEY MAY NEVER KNOW THE DUST

PART ONE

SARAH

It was such a perfect day, a promise of summer with cloudless blue skies. Swallows were nesting below the eaves of the janitor's cottage, and out on the sports field the tenth graders were playing cricket and tennis. Everyone thought, when the alarm bell rang, that it was just another fire drill. But the first bombs had fallen on Hamburg and Leningrad, the headmaster said, and a full-scale nuclear attack was imminent. Those within walking distance of the school must go home immediately. The rest would return to the main assembly hall and stay there.

Sarah ran through a town gone mad with panic. The traffic had stopped . . . cars and trucks parked all along the narrow main street. Men and women, crazy with fear, looted the shops for supplies. Police sirens sounded, and in the housing development they were tearing doors from their hinges to board up the windows. Sarah's school shoes pounded along the pavements, up the hill past the district hospital, leaving the town behind. A stitch in her side and her lungs heaving for breath made her stop and look back.

She saw the streets spread out beneath her, the river estuary shining silver in the distance, white piles of the nuclear power station on the opposite bank, and the Cotswold Hills beyond. She had to remember it . . . Gloucestershire green in the sunlight, a black-bird singing, and the wind blowing warm through her hair. With all her senses she had to remember it, all the scents and sights and sounds of a world she might never see again. The roadside was lacy with cow parsley, and May had covered the hedges with sweet white blossoms. Cattle grazed in the fields. A kestrel hovered, and the woods were dreamy with bluebells. She heard a cuckoo calling through the silence. She heard the others running along the roadway ahead. Their voices called to her.

"Hurry up! You haven't time to stop!"

Sarah covered two miles in twenty minutes.

Scattered houses marked the village outskirts, with Monday laundry billowing in the gardens. And over the hill the church bell tolled. Sarah's home was in a hollow, two renovated cottages made into one. There were lawns in front and borders bright with flowers and an orchard at the back. She entered through the kitchen. Buster barked and wagged his tail in greeting, but she paid him no heed. She went into the living room, where her stepmother was nailing a blanket over the window.

"Is it true?" Sarah gasped.

"Don't ask stupid questions!" Veronica snapped.

But the nuclear war was a million miles away. Hamburg was in Germany, Sarah said, and this was England. She could not believe that anyone would drop atomic bombs on England. They already had, Veronica informed her. The B.B.C. had stopped transmitting a few minutes ago, and Radio Bristol reported London had been hit.

Stay in your houses, the announcer said.

"Give me a hand," Veronica said grimly.

Sarah helped her drag the mattress from the double bed and drag it downstairs. They took the spare one from the guest room and wedged both against the window, shifted the sideboard to hold them in place, and stacked the bookcase on top. It was what the radio announcer told them to do as protection against flying glass. Daylight came in through the open doors, but the room was dark, and Sarah turned on the light.

"Will Daddy be home?" she asked.

"Use your head!" Veronica retorted.

Sarah bit her lip.

Her father was teaching at Bristol University and would not have time to drive home. And Veronica did not mean to be unkind. She was doing everything she could to keep herself and the children alive, and she did not have time to think of Sarah's father.

Gather all necessary belongings into one room, instructed the radio announcer. *Seal the doors against nuclear fallout.*

The door to the kitchen still remained open, but Veronica sealed the door to the hall with adhesive tape. There was nothing left for Sarah to do. In the gloomy light she saw canned food piled in a corner, bowls and buckets filled with water, the camping stove and gas cylinder brought in from the garage, half a sack of potatoes, and Grandma's commode. The settee was piled with clothes and bedclothes, pillows and cushions, books and cups and saucepans, plastic garbage bags, Catherine's Barbie doll and William's Tonka truck.

William and Catherine, who had returned from the village school long before Sarah had come home, had made a camp under the dining table, draped with blankets and boxed in with mattresses from their own and Sarah's beds. They laughed and giggled and thought it was fun. And Buster was under there with them, yelping and barking in some rough-and-tumble game.

"Get that dog out of here!" Veronica told Sarah.

It was a terrible thing to do. William screamed and clung to him. He was only five and did not understand . . . they might have to stay indoors for weeks, everyone shut inside the living room and never going out. They could not have Buster with them. They would probably have to eat his dog food, and they might even have to eat Buster himself. On her hands and knees Sarah crawled beneath the table and dragged the dog from William's arms.

"He'll be all right," she said consolingly. "He can catch rabbits, and it might only be for a little while. Mommy doesn't want him to pee on the carpet, that's all."

She carried Buster outside and set him down, watched him frisk across the orchard. She had to remember . . . a fat cocker spaniel in the last bright moments of life . . . sunlight among apple leaves, a scent of wallflowers and the massed colors of polyanthus. She had to remember the stand of larches beyond the orchard wall, sheep bleating on the common, and the church bell tolling . . . *dong* . . . *dong* . . . *dong*.

Sarah looked up at the blue heavenly sky. In the end people turned to God. But the death that would come had nothing to do with Him. He, and the world, and the whole of creation, were about to be destroyed. Away to the north she heard a rumble of thunder, or maybe a nuclear explosion. It did not matter which. Nothing mattered anymore. Up from the river the seagulls drifted like scraps of blown paper. Their bird voices screamed as she wanted to scream—scream out her anger and despair, the single word, the one almighty question . . . why?

Catherine came running from the house.

"Birmingham! Birmingham!" Catherine shouted. "Mommy says Birmingham has been hit and you're to come inside!" She stopped and touched Sarah's arm. "Oh look, there's a butterfly," she said.

It was a small tortoiseshell sunning its wings on a clump of purple aubrietia. It was the last thing Sarah saw—a butterfly among flowers and Buster's brown doggy eyes laughing at her from the shadows of the apple orchard—before she went inside and closed the door.

∘∘∘

When Sarah closed the kitchen door, the last of the daylight was shut out, and Veronica went to work with the adhesive tape. Already the room felt like a prison. The electric light seemed gloomy and unreal, the atmosphere hot and stuffy. Veronica pushed newspaper into the keyhole, and the voice of the radio announcer droned on.

Stay where you are. Remain in your houses. Close all doors and windows. Secure one room against fall-out and flying glass. Dangerous contamination is expected for the next fourteen days. Do not go outside until you are told it is safe to do so. There will be further broadcasts throughout this period.

Sarah stopped listening. She sat on a dining chair, chewing her fingernails, and wishing her father would come home.

"Stop doing that!" Veronica said angrily.

Guiltily Sarah stopped.

Remain in your houses, said the radio announcer.

"*This* is my house," Catherine said from beneath the table. "I'm going to live in it forever and ever. And you can, William."

"What about my tea?" said William.

"We can have tea here," said Catherine. "*And* dinner and supper. The man says we mustn't go out at all."

"Suppose I want to go to the toilet?" said William.

"Mommy says we have to go on the commode."

"*And* Sarah?"

Sarah felt sick at the thought of it. They would have to live with the stink, all of them together in the closed room. A few flies buzzed around the lampshade and Veronica's lips twisted in distaste. Like Sarah, she realized their sanitary arrangements were totally inadequate, but it was too late now to fetch the disinfectant from the bathroom.

Remain in your houses, the radio announcer repeated. *Do not go outside until you are told it is safe to do so.*

Then, quite suddenly, his monotonous voice stopped talking. And a few minutes later the lights went out.

"This is it," Veronica said grimly.

"Bristol?" asked Sarah.

"It's all dark!" Catherine shrieked. "I don't like it! I want to be with you, Mommy!"

"Stay where you are!" Veronica said urgently. "Sarah and I are right here in the room, and the dark won't hurt you. You must stay under the table and look after William."

"I'm not afraid of the dark," William said scornfully.

"Then look after Catherine," Veronica said.

Sarah's whole body was tense and listening. It was very dark in the room, but a faint line of sunlight showed through the weave of the blanket at the top of the window. She heard a rumble in the distance, a great wave of sound that came sweeping toward her, engulfing everything in its path, drowning Catherine's cries. Sarah blundered toward the fragile edge of light as the blast struck the house.

Roof tiles smashed and the windows were blown inward. Books and ornaments and light fixtures crashed and fell in the upstairs rooms. In the howling darkness the mattresses sagged, and the bookcase started to topple. The black human shape that was Veronica screamed at her to help. But Sarah was already there, moved by her instinct, exerting force against force. The blanket tore at its nails, came loose at one corner. Heat screamed through the crack. Sarah had one brief glimpse of devastation, a hurricane of tearing trees and whirling leaves, the sky turned dark and lurid with fire, before the wind passed over them and things sank back into stillness.

Catherine was sobbing beneath the table.

Fragments of glass slipped and fell.

The air was stifling.

"Is it over?" Sarah asked.

"That was just the beginning," Veronica said brutally.

"We don't stand a chance!" Sarah cried.

"There's a flashlight on the mantelpiece!" Veronica told her. "And the hammer is beside it. I'll need some nails too. Hurry up!"

Veronica removed the bookcase and nailed the blanket back into place. They had to have something heavier, she said, and between them they managed to lift the settee on top of the sideboard. It was made of leather and horsehair, and its carved legs hooked over the back. Bed sheets and blankets were jammed into the space along the top as the next wave of sound came screaming toward them.

They applied their shoulders, all the strength they had, to hold the sofa in place as the bombs fell over Bristol and Cardiff and Cheltenham, and the great winds followed, a roaring tide of heat and darkness that smashed like a gigantic fist against the house. Even through the thickness of the walls Sarah seemed to see it . . . hell-bright hues, impressions of colors that flashed and pulsed, rose and gold and red-vermillion, impaled on her eyes as the wind screamed through the broken upstairs windows and the barricade shuddered. Wave after wave of thundering sound beat at the doors and walls of their sanctuary, until it faded away into silence.

They listened and waited. Buster was howling outside, and in the hallway the grandfather clock struck
four, a silly incongruous sound. It had been a very
short war, and they heard nothing more.

"I guess it's over," Veronica said.

"Bristol?" asked Sarah.

"Everything," Veronica replied.

Sarah let go. She was weak and shaking. There was
a pain in her shoulder where the wooden frame of the
settee had cut into her flesh, and her hands hurt so
much she could hardly bear it. She sat in the dark on
the dining chair, biting her lip.

Veronica turned on the flashlight.

"Are you all right?"

Sarah wanted to cry, weep like a small child, pretend
Veronica was her mother, cling to her for comfort as
William and Catherine always did. But she and Veronica had never been close. She was just the woman
her father had married, mother of William and Catherine, but nothing to do with Sarah.

"Do you think Daddy's still alive?" she asked.

"If he is," said Veronica, "he won't be able to come
to us. There's no point in hoping, Sarah. We're on our
own."

"We don't even like each other very much," Sarah
mourned.

"Then I suggest we start," Veronica said crisply.
"Because all we have is each other."

Sarah bent her head.

Slow tears trickled down her cheeks.

"I can't bear it," she said.

"I want my tea," said William.

"What about Buster?" Catherine sobbed.

"And 'this is the way the world ends,' " Veronica murmured. " 'Not with a bang, but a whimper.' "

◦◦◦

That first evening was strange and special, as if it were someone's birthday, a change from the usual household routine. They ate by candlelight—fish sticks, crinkle-cut french fries, and green beans, with thawing ice cream for dessert . . . food that Veronica had taken from the freezer and had to be used up quickly. Water was precious and could not be used for doing dishes, so they wiped their plates clean with paper tissues, which they threw into the empty fire grate. Milk also would not keep for long. Veronica made custard, filled a thermos of cocoa for later to save on the gas, and stood the remaining two pints in a bowl of water to prevent it going sour overnight.

Afterward they played guessing games and Sarah read fairy stories by Hans Christian Andersen. They tried not to listen to Buster whining outside the window, his claws scratching at the woodwork, begging to come in. Veronica said he had to stay out there, so they all sang songs to help William forget, their voices drowning the pitiful doggy sounds he made. But always, in the background, Buster remained. And the candle lasted only four hours.

It was half past eight by Sarah's digital watch, green luminous time ticking away the seconds as Buster scrabbled and whined. They must all go to bed, Veronica said, because there were only twelve candles in the pack and they could not use more than one a day. In the yellow beam of the flashlight they made up beds on the floor—William and Catherine on a mattress under the table, and Sarah in the space by the hall door. They heaved the settee from the sideboard for Veronica to sleep on, and the room snapped back into darkness.

"We haven't washed," said Catherine. "Or cleaned our teeth."

"You can be excused for tonight," Veronica said.

"Can we be excused tomorrow as well?" Catherine asked.

"Yes," said Veronica. "Now go to sleep."

It was a hot still night, windless and quiet. Nine o'clock by Sarah's watch and probably still light outside. Unless it was dark, she thought, like Good Friday when Christ was crucified and the skies turned black reflecting the evil of mankind. She imagined the darkness covering the earth, a world where the sun ceased to rise and nothing lived, or grew, or flowered. She imagined the dust of fallout blowing across the ruins of their civilization, burying buildings and people. It was a terrible punishment for a fifteen-year-old girl who had done nothing wrong.

Catherine and William whispered and giggled beneath the table, but then Buster returned to whine under the window again. He wanted his supper, William said, and demanded he be let in. Veronica tried to explain. One night without supper would not hurt him. He was too fat anyway. Maybe tomorrow they would let him in. But William went on asking, his small boy's voice growing querulous and tearful in the darkness. Finally Veronica shouted at Buster, loudly and angrily, told him to go and lie down. Her tone must have reached him, for they heard nothing more . . . only

William muttering and crying, saying how cruel and horrible Veronica was. He was going to report her to the R.S.P.C.A., but after a while he too fell silent.

"William's asleep," Catherine announced.

"So why aren't you?" Veronica asked her.

She wanted to use the commode. Veronica put a large saucepan lid over it, but the smell was still there, strong and obnoxious, lingering in the room. They would not be able to live with it, Sarah thought. They would not be able to live in the stinking perpetual dark with nothing to do and only a few hours of candlelight a day, four people trapped in one room and two of them children. William and Catherine would not be content with sitting still for the next two weeks, just thinking and talking and playing games with their minds. They would more likely drive each other mad.

"Veronica?" Sarah said quietly. "What are we going to do?"

"Go to sleep," Veronica muttered.

"I'm not a baby!" Sarah retorted. "We've got to talk."

"Not in front of Catherine."

"She's asleep. I can hear her breathing. We'll never stand living like this, Veronica. We've got to have some sort of plan."

"What do you suggest?" Veronica asked her.

"I don't know."

"Then we'll have to manage as best we can. Live each day at a time and try not to think of it."

"We'd be better off dead!" Sarah said bitterly.

"Don't talk like that," Veronica begged.

"It's true!" said Sarah. "There's only one thing worse than dying in a nuclear war, and that's surviving! We

haven't started yet! Even if we live through the next
fourteen days, there will be nothing left at the end of
it—just ruins and radiation sickness . . . no one to help
us, no means of living. Even the soil and water will
be contaminated! We'll die anyway, so what's the point
of trying to survive now?"

"What's the alternative?"

"We could get something from the drugstore."

"Commit suicide, you mean? Is that what you want
to do?"

"Don't you?" Sarah asked.

Veronica sighed.

"If it were only myself, I think I wouldn't hesitate.
But I've Catherine and William to consider. It mightn't
be as bad as we think, and they might still have a
future. I've got no right to take it away, Sarah."

"What about me?" Sarah asked.

"I can't answer for you," said Veronica.

Sarah chewed her fingernails. A sick heavy feeling
lodged in her stomach, a dull acceptance that was worse
than fear. She sensed that the future held no hope, at
least not for herself. But Veronica was compelled to
live for the sake of William and Catherine, and so too
was Sarah, because that was the only purpose she had
left.

∘∘∘

Sarah awoke in the stinking stifling dark to the sound
of Buster howling around the walls and William asking
to get up. It was not time, Veronica said. But Sarah's
watch showed ten minutes past ten. It was Tuesday
morning, the late beginning of another day, and

Veronica was trying to delay the start of it. "Go back to sleep!" she said curtly. But William had slept already for thirteen hours and would not sleep again, not with Buster yelping outside.

"He wants his breakfast!" William said angrily.

"And I do," said Catherine.

"We have to get up sometime," Sarah said.

Veronica turned on the flashlight. In her crumpled clothes and disheveled hair she rose from the settee and crossed the messes on the floor. There were tear-stains on her face, and reflections shone on the blank television screen. A photograph of Sarah's father watched from the mantelpiece as she washed in a bucket of cold water and ran a comb through the tangles of her hair. Then she lit the second candle, turned off the flashlight, and lifted the blanket that draped the table.

"All right, you can come out now. Wash your faces and hands in the end bucket and find something to wear."

"You said we didn't have to wash," Catherine reminded her.

"So get yourself dressed then."

"I want to stay in my house."

"You can't stay in there all day!"

"I shall stay in here forever and ever," Catherine said stubbornly.

"*I'm* going to let Buster in," said William.

"You're to leave him where he is!" Veronica snapped.

"You said he could come in!" William argued. "Tomorrow, you said. And this *is* tomorrow!"

"He can come in later," Veronica promised.

"I want him to come in *now!*"

William stamped his foot.

"Do as I tell you!" Veronica scolded. "And come away from that door!"

"I hate you!" William screeched.

Sarah wiped her face with a wet washcloth and pulled on her jeans and a T-shirt, as Veronica cooked bacon and sausages and sliced tomatoes over the camping stove. Already the situation was beginning to get on Veronica's nerves. Catherine behaved well. She tidied her house under the table, made a tablecloth with a spread-out newspaper, and ate her breakfast with two slices of bread and a mug of tea. But William refused to change from his pajamas. He sat and sulked in the corner by the sofa as Buster howled outside and the sausages and bacon congealed on his plate.

"I don't want no breakfast!" William said savagely. "If Buster's not having any then I'm not having any neither! So there! And you'll be sorry then when I'm starved to death!"

"Don't count on it!" Veronica said brutally.

Someone had to get through to William. Someone had to explain about Buster and persuade him to eat. But Veronica was in one of her moods, brooding and silent, eating her breakfast at the far end of the settee. It had to be Sarah. It had to be Sarah who put aside everything she felt, who dug deeper than grief or worry into the still quiet center of herself, and did what Veronica could not.

She sat on the floor beside her small half brother and took him in her arms. He was the only reason she would go on living and she gave him all she had . . . her pity, her comfort and her love. And perhaps she had never loved William before, but she loved him then. And she told him what he needed to know. Outside there was dust, falling like snow, and if they opened the door to let Buster in, the dust would come in too, and kill them. He had to be brave and strong, do what Veronica asked, and eat his breakfast.

"Will the dust kill Buster?" William inquired.

"Yes," said Sarah.

"Why tell him that?" Veronica said angrily.

"Because it's true," said Sarah. "And he has to know."

It was odd how easily William accepted that Buster was going to die. How he could talk of it without tears or emotion and eat his breakfast as he did so. And when the room snuffed back into darkness it was William who shouted.

"Go away, Buster! You can't come in!"

"Poor little Buster," Catherine sobbed.

"Jesus will look after him," Veronica told her.

Jesus would not give him food and water, Sarah thought. Nor could she and Veronica sit there and let Buster die. Not even Veronica could be that uncaring. Underneath she would be feeling it, suffering it, the slow sad lingering hours and days of Buster's life. Sarah knew that in the end she would give in and go outside. For a gold cocker spaniel Veronica would die.

And then Sarah would be left alone to keep William and Catherine alive, foraging among the ruins of the village when their food supplies ran out. She tried not to think of it, but in the hot dark room there was nothing else to do but think. She could find in her thoughts no hope or consolation, but neither did she dread the time that was to come. Perhaps she was gone beyond fear. That moment when she had taken William in her arms had awakened something inside her—a calm and strength such as she had never known before. She felt there was something in her own being that nothing could destroy, that whatever occurred, however terrible, Sarah knew she could bear it.

ᴏ–ᴏ–ᴏ

There was nothing left that Sarah could want for herself, or even hope for. What remained of her life belonged to them . . . to William and Catherine and Veronica, people trapped with her in the wailing, whining, grieving, bickering dark. She was adrift in a black sea of time, awaiting her cue to placate, or comfort, or mediate. Knowing how to pity, she did not need to forgive—the stench of human excrement, Buster's sad doggy song going on and on, William's anger and frustration, and Veronica's moods of violence and despair.

"*Why* can't I watch television?" William asked.

"Because there's no electricity!" Veronica snapped. "How many more times do I have to tell you?"

"Then why don't you turn the lights on?" William said furiously. "Then we'll have electricity, won't we? And I can watch television then!"

Sarah tried to explain. She told him about power stations and power lines and the effects of nuclear war. There were no utilities . . . no lights, no water, no television; no schools, no hospitals, and no delivery trucks. The world as they had known it was gone. William listened and questioned and finally, in his own five-year-old language, he understood. There would be no chocolate bars, no Atari space games, no trips to the supermarket, no cowboy films, no birthday parties, and no Father Christmas, ever again. Just ruins and dust, cold baked beans for dinner when the gas ran out, and twelve more days of almost total darkness. And not even Veronica could change things, Sarah said. She might be his mother, and she might be grown up, but she could not put things right.

"So you mustn't blame her because you can't watch television," Sarah reasoned.

For several minutes William thought of it.

"In the dark," he concluded, "you can't do nothing much."

"Blind people can," Catherine said smugly.

"Blind people have white sticks!" William said scornfully.

"Not all of them," said Catherine. "Mrs. Wetherby doesn't, and she can do most things. If we were blind we could do most things too. We could find your Tonka truck, William. And my Barbie doll."

Sarah held her breath. Catherine was only eight, but her child's imagination had seen a way to live in the dark without eyes. They did not have to be helpless. They could hear sounds, distinguish things by touch. They could restore order to the chaos of the room, clear the floor, and learn to move about. They could play the blind game. It would give them a purpose, fill the empty hours between one meal and the next. And a stake from the potted begonia could be William's white stick.

"Listen!" said Sarah. "We're going to play the blind game."

Veronica said she was not in the mood to play games, but she did tell them what to do, her voice organizing their activity. They emptied the cardboard box of the last of the freezer food, packed it full of glass and

crystal from the sideboard that they would never use
again, and stowed it in the corner behind the easy chair
along with the contents of the drawers. The drawers
were used for socks and underwear, and the sideboard
shelves were used for storing clothes, everything neatly
folded and put away. All the unnecessary things the
room contained were also dumped in the corner—vases
and ornaments, the magazine rack, books and the reading lamp, and the silver coffee set Aunt Maud had
given for a wedding present. The bookcase became a
pantry and Catherine arranged the cans on the shelves,
stacked saucepans and crockery along the top. They
moved Sarah's bed behind the settee and made a toilet
in the alcove by the hall door. William and Sarah between them hammered nails into the wall, made a line
with a piece of string, and hung a blanket over it,
hoping it would hide the smell.

When they relit the second candle, the room looked
strange and tidy: dining chairs stacked on the sideboard, the furniture moved to unfamiliar places around
the walls, a central space, and private shadowy ter-
ritories. William, who had an apartment in the second
easy chair, sat fiddling with the wheels of his Tonka
truck as Veronica cooked beefburgers, peas, and the
rest of the crinkle-cut potatoes. They had cold custard
and a carton of thawed raspberries for dessert.

It was an amalgamation of tea and dinner, the grandfather clock striking five on a May afternoon. But time
and seasons had lost their meaning. They ate because
they were hungry, and it might have been winter in
the darkness and candlelight and stuffy inside warmth.
They even lit a fire, burned the trash collected in the
hearth, the litter of civilized prepackaging and paper

tissues. For a while the room was bright and cheerful until the last flame died. Then they were back in the darkness again, each one sitting alone in their allotted places.

"*I'm* in my house," said Catherine.

"*I'm* in my apartment," said William.

"Where are you, Mommy?" Catherine asked.

"Blackpool beach," Veronica said wearily.

Sarah was sitting on her bed behind the sofa.

And the grandfather clock chimed six.

"We ought to start food rationing tomorrow," Sarah said. "And we could do with a proper wash."

"Body smells and dirty clothes," Veronica murmured. "What's the point in trying to keep up civilized standards?"

William's Tonka truck zoomed across the carpet.

"I haven't heard Buster for ages," said William.

"I expect he's dead," said Catherine matter-of-factly.

"Not already," Sarah said firmly.

"He must be asleep somewhere," Veronica said.

"Or dying of hunger," William said.

"What will you do about him?" Sarah asked.

Veronica made no answer.

"You'll go and see to him, won't you?"

"I can't just leave him to die," Veronica said.

"Will you go now? Today?"

Veronica sighed.

"I'll go tomorrow," she said. "Starvation won't hurt him for one more night."

Perhaps, Sarah thought, it was something to look forward to, Veronica going outside. It would make their isolation easier to bear knowing the world was still there, seeing the trees and the houses. It would

help them to realize there were others like themselves . . . fat Mrs. Porter across the common, the
Spencers in Brookside Cottage, Harrowgate Farm on
top of the hill. There would be flowers still blooming
in the garden, leaves on the apple trees, birds perhaps,
and animals. Because, of course, the world had not yet
ended. It would die gradually, just as they would, and
perhaps through Veronica's eyes they would see it
again before its beauty was gone.

ooo

When the candle was lit to mark the beginning of another day, Sarah took the sewing basket from under
the television table. She made a pair of bloomers from
a black plastic garbage bag, with shirring elastic at
the waist and legs. She made a tunic with elasticized
sleeves from a second garbage bag, and from a third
she made a pair of oversocks which reached above
Veronica's knees. Her body was completely covered.
A transparent freezer bag with pinprick holes to let
in the air made a helmet, and there were rubber gloves
in the kitchen drawer. Dressed in her makeshift protective clothing, Veronica made ready to go outside,
and Sarah peeled away the adhesive tape from around
the door.

"You'd better go under the table with William and
Catherine," Veronica told her.

Sarah nodded, blew out the candle, and crawled into
the stifling blanketed darkness of Catherine's house.
How Catherine could stay under there for hour after
hour was quite beyond her. She thought she would
suffocate with every breath. She could feel the heat

of William's body beside her as she listened to the
opening and closing of the door, the shuffle of footsteps
across the kitchen, and the rattle of the safety chain.
Muffled by walls came Buster's joyful greeting, whim-
pering and whining, and Veronica's indistinguishable
replies.

"I want to see Buster too!" said William. "You could
make me a garbage-bag suit, Sarah. There's one behind the chair. We could empty the things and I could
go with Mommy."

"It's too dangerous," Sarah told him.

"Little boys have to stay inside," Catherine said
crushingly.

"I'm *not* a little boy!" William said furiously.

"Listen!" said Sarah.

They could hear Veronica walking around outside
the house. The lid of the rain barrel clattered as she
gave Buster water. There were sounds from the garage and garden tools falling, Veronica coming back
to the house and calling to Sarah . . . but William was
at the door before her, and gray daylight flooded the
room.

"Can we come out?" William asked eagerly.

"Go back under that table!" Veronica said savagely.

Sarah pushed William behind her, closed the door
to a crack. He screamed and pummeled her, but she
would not let him pass. Finally she spanked him, hard
around the legs, and sent him screaming into the dark
far recesses of the room.

"Sarah hit me, Mommy!"

"When I come in I'll give you another!" Veronica
told him. "Take hold of this," she said to Sarah.

It was meat from the freezer that had not yet gone bad . . . beef and liver and two packs of sodden vegetables. Veronica also said she would bury the contents of the commode while she was outside, and if Sarah would give her the front-door key from her purse, she would fetch disinfectant from the bathroom and the air-freshener spray.

Veronica came and went as William went on with his tantrum. Sarah heard water flush from the tap and the clink of china. She heard her moving through the upstairs rooms, and Buster whining in the kitchen, but she would not let him into the room for all William screamed. Finally Veronica returned, took off her garbage-bag clothes, and reentered the darkness. She had brought the Lego bricks for William to play with and clothes for Catherine's Barbie doll, and the room smelled strong and sweet with bouquet of pine.

"What was it like outside?" Sarah asked her.

It was gray, said Veronica. Gray and eerie . . . semi-darkness, and a windless silence like the hush before the storm. Only the storm had already happened—flowers battered and broken, trees uprooted in the stand of larches, the roof gone from Mrs. Porter's house, and trailing telephone wires. And the darkness was not cloud, Veronica said. It was dust. Dust falling over everything, gray on the grass, and the rhubarb leaves, and the surface of the water in the rain barrel.

"Depressing," said Veronica. "Horrible and depressing."

It was radioactive fallout, Sarah thought. In a few days everything would be dead, plant life and animal life choked by the dust, and Buster would not live long.

Sarah almost wished that Veronica had not gone outside. She had wanted to hear about sunlight and flowers, not reality and radioactive dust.

Time passed long and grueling, filled with intima-
tions of death, and William plagued them worse than
boredom. He was driving Veronica mad with his whining and grumbling and incessant complaints. Catherine
used the Lego bricks to build furniture for her Barbie
doll, and there was nothing for Sarah to do except help
Veronica prepare for the next meal.

Using only their sense of touch, they cut the joint
of beef into tiny fragments, diced carrots and onions,
added salt and pepper, half a bouillon cube, and a pint
of water, and set it to stew on the camping stove. The
flame of the burner shed a small blue light, enough to
distinguish the shapes of things, and the smell of cooking grew savory and strong. Every two minutes William asked if it was ready. But the stew was for
tomorrow, Veronica said. He had to wait until it was
cooked, then wait again while she fried the liver and
onions and boiled a bag of mixed vegetables.

Then William complained that the drinking water
tasted funny and made his teeth go all gritty. It was
stale and flat in an open bucket and Catherine refused
to drink it.

"Have some from the plastic container?" Sarah suggested. "It might taste better."

"But is it *safe* water?" Catherine asked.

"What do you mean?" Sarah asked curiously.

"You said everything's constipated and if we eat it
we'll die."

"Contaminated," said Sarah.

"So I don't want any," Catherine stated.

"There's no way this water can be contaminated," Sarah assured her. "It's got a screw top."

"Then I'll have some," said Catherine.

Sarah poured water from the container into her beaker. Catherine was a strange child, she thought, unusually compliant, never complaining, yet cautious of everything. For hours on end she had sat in the dark of her house below the table, determined to stay there for as long as she had to. It was as if she sensed it was the surest way to stay alive. From a busy, bossy, organizing little girl, Catherine had changed into a child who was remote and self-sufficient, not questioning what anyone did unless it directly concerned her. In her odd adult voice she inquired if the water was safe, making sure, obeying an instinct. And suddenly Sarah realized. Whatever happened to herself and William and Veronica, Catherine intended to survive.

∘∘∘

It was Saturday, or maybe only Friday. Sarah was not sure. They had stayed in their beds not wanting it to begin, hoping William would sleep right through until midnight. But he had woken at a quarter to twelve, hardly midday, and Sarah had lit the candle and set the kettle to boil. Now he waited, naked on the hearth rug, as she poured hot water into a bowl. They had to wash and put on clean clothes, Sarah said.

"And Catherine?" said William.

"Everyone," said Sarah.

"And Mommy?"

"Mommy isn't feeling very well."

"We shouldn't talk to her?" Catherine whispered.

"Best if you don't," said Sarah. "She wants to be left alone."

In the same bowl of water Sarah washed William and Catherine, and then herself. Briefly it made her feel better, fresh and clean, restoring her sense of well-being. She could almost believe that today would be good and so would William. She mixed powdered milk for the cornflakes and fed them the last slices of bread spread with butter and strawberry jam. Veronica shook her head. She was going without so that they could have more, living on black coffee and one meal a day. Sarah wiped the jam from William's fingers.

"I'm still hungry," he announced.

"You've had your rations," Sarah told him.

"But I'm still *hungry!*"

Sarah put a handful of dog biscuits into his empty cornflake dish. It was a large three-kilo bag that had hardly been started and would last for days. William said they tasted quite nice, so Catherine had some too, helped herself and carefully resealed the bag before retiring to her house underneath the table. Using the same bowl of water they had washed in, Sarah washed the plates and mugs they had used over and over for the last few days, scrubbed away the grimed-on grease and gravy.

"I'm going to blow out the candle now," she said.

Black despair showed briefly in Veronica's eyes.

And was instantly extinguished.

The long hours of darkness had begun again.

"What are we having for dinner?" William asked.

"Stew," said Catherine. "The same as yesterday and the day before."

"It's got to be used up," said Sarah. "I'll add some more potatoes."

William crunched the hard lumps of dog biscuit.

"I want real dinner," he said. "I want custard and beefburgers and french fries and strawberry ice cream. Tell Sarah to get me a real dinner, Mommy!"

"Mommy?" said Catherine. "Are you going to feed Buster today?"

"I'll do it," Sarah said grimly.

"No," Veronica said dully. "I'll go."

She moved apathetically, groped her way across the room, and peeled away the adhesive tape from around the door. She did not order William to go under the table. It was as if she no longer cared if he lived or died. A rectangle of gloomy twilight showed briefly and was gone, and Sarah listened to the rustle of the garbage-bag clothes as Veronica put them on.

Buster must have been waiting outside the door, but his greeting was subdued and Veronica hardly spoke to him. She said, when she returned, that he did not seem interested in food, and the meat in the freezer had all gone bad. She seemed more dispirited than ever, gripped by a hopelessness from which she could not escape. And the world outside was semidark, smothered by dust, everything green turned gray. She had seen dead sheep lying on the common and she had not emptied the commode.

"If the sheep are dead," said William, "we could have one for dinner."

"No," said Sarah. "They died of radiation sickness."

"And we'll die too if we eat them," said Catherine.

"I'm fed up with stew," said William.

"You can have dog biscuits instead," said Sarah.

"I've just *had* dog biscuits!" William said furiously. He threw the empty dish into the fire grate.

And it was one more temper tantrum for Sarah to deal with, one more irrational incident to add to the madness of yesterday. "Why doesn't he understand?" Veronica said desperately. But William would never understand.

He roamed through the darkness, aimless and irksome, a five-year-old child dependent on sounds to keep him interested, and the sounds alone were enough to drive anyone crazy. He lifted the bucket handle and let it clatter back into place, over and over again, until Sarah shouted at him to stop it. Then he made chimes with the begonia stick on the fireside companion set, a metallic music as the tongs and brush, poker and shovel, rattled and clanged. Sarah removed them and stowed them in the corner with the rest of the junk. After that William played with the switches on the television, changing channels with loud irritating clicks, ignoring Sarah when she asked him not to, waiting for his mother. And the reaction came, the same as yesterday.

"I'm going to kill you in a minute!" Veronica screamed. "I'll smash your head against the wall! Leave that flaming television alone!"

William retreated to the armchair, drummed his heels against the side. He talked about dinner, whined and grumbled, wanted a pack of potato chips, wanted ginger cake and chocolate bars and an orange ice pop. Everything Veronica could not give him William wanted and demanded to know why. Deprivation was something he had never known before, and Veronica had always been his main source of supply. He refused to accept that what she had always given him she could give him no longer. In a fit of rage he broke up Catherine's Barbie doll furniture and hurled it into the blind dark space where Veronica sat.

"You buy me a chocolate bar, Mommy!" William shouted.

Nobody expected Veronica to cry but she cried then, long broken sobs that racked her body, a human sound of absolute despair. William was shocked into silence and Catherine, who had been screaming at him for breaking her Barbie doll furniture, was silent too. Sarah groped her way toward the settee, feeling the debris of Lego bricks, not knowing what to do or say. She touched Veronica's leg, her hand, her shoulder. Put her arms around the older woman she had never loved.

"Don't cry," said Sarah. "Don't cry, Veronica. William didn't mean it. He didn't mean to hurt you. He's only a little boy and he doesn't understand."

"Oh, God!" Veronica wept. "I can't go on like this. I just can't. It's not only William. It's everything. All of us trapped in this hellhole of a room. I can't stand it! I just can't stand it any longer!"

"It's only for another eight or nine days," Sarah said consolingly.

"You haven't been outside!" Veronica sobbed. "You don't know what it's like. Everything's dying. There's no way we'll be able to stay alive. Nothing to hope for. No future for any of us. I should have listened to you. I should have gone to the drugstore and gotten some pills."

"No," said Sarah. "There's William and Catherine,

remember? We can't give up, Veronica. We've got to think about them, do everything we can to help them stay alive."

"I can't!" said Veronica. "I can't go on! I can't even try! It's pointless, Sarah. Completely pointless!"

Sarah stood up.

It had to be her. She would have to take on the responsibility Veronica abandoned. Their lives in her hands. It was a huge undertaking, but she could feel the strength inside her like a great welling of power. She was not alone. In the hushed darkness around her she could feel a presence, sense the eternal being of which she was a part. She knew it was all for a purpose, that she had to go on. Something in the future was dependent on her. And although she might die, something or someone would survive because of her, and God himself would give her courage.

ooo

After Veronica broke down, William behaved better. Through the long dark hours he played with Catherine and the Lego bricks, children's voices talking quietly together. Veronica said nothing more. She seemed to be withdrawn inside herself, sunk into a kind of torpor, not knowing or caring what went on. Sarah reheated the stew and William ate it without complaint. But Veronica lay on the sofa, refusing to eat or drink. All she had had all day was a cup of black coffee. It was as if she had lost the will to live, and Sarah was afraid to press her.

She put the saucepan to soak in the bowl of filthy water and wiped the plates clean with crumpled newspaper. The fire grate was full of rubbish—biscuit wrappings, tissues, and the empty cornflakes box. Candlelight flickered and a match flared brightly as she bent to set it on fire

It was then that Sarah noticed . . . there was dust in the hearth, gray dust falling like soot, silent and deadly. She blew out the match and turned on the flashlight, shone it around the room. The dust was everywhere, on all the surfaces, floating like scum on the bucket of drinking water. Is it safe? Catherine had asked, as if she had suspected it was not. And the dust was inside them now, in herself and William and Veronica, inside their gullets and being absorbed. They had guarded against fallout as the radio announcer had said, but they had forgotten to block up the chimney, which was open to the sky.

"Veronica!" Sarah said urgently. "This water's contaminated!"

Veronica raised her head.

Dead eyes stared at Sarah, uncomprehendingly.

Sarah ran her finger along the mantelpiece.

And thrust it under her nose.

"Dust!" said Sarah. "Look at it!"

Veronica stared.

Her blue eyes flickered.

And she understood.

"Where's it coming from?" she asked in alarm.

"Down the chimney," Sarah told her. "I'll find something to block it up. We're going to have to clean this room. We'll have to wash everything with disinfectant, and we'll need some more drinking water. You'll have to go and get some. The hot-water tap should be all right, as it's a closed-in cylinder . . . and I'll need the carpet sweeper and a bottle of carpet shampoo."

Veronica stood up.

Suddenly her face displayed purpose.

And her voice was calm and controlled.

"Go under the table, William," she said. "And stay under there until I've fetched the things we need."

"I want to help," said William.

"You can help when I come back," Veronica said.

"Will I have to help too?" Catherine asked worriedly.

"I think we can manage," said Sarah.

"But there might be dust in my house! And I breathed it when I came out! Am I going to die now?"

"I shouldn't think so," Sarah said.

The grandfather clock struck nine before they had finished. The day's candle had burned away, and Sarah had lit another. The room smelled sweeter . . . disinfectant, furniture polish, and carpet shampoo, stronger than the stink of human excrement and stale stew. William had washed the bookcase. The food cans were polished and shiny and the junk was gone from the corner behind the chair. Even the soiled clothes and the dining chairs Veronica had taken outside and dumped in the garage. And she said Buster seemed a little brighter. He had drunk all his water and eaten the meat from his dish, unless it was rats. Veronica had seen the rats gnawing at the body of a dead sheep, and she carried a poker when she went outside to empty the commode.

Sarah used new lengths of adhesive tape to reseal the door, and William filled a beaker with fresh water from the bucket. Candlelight flickered, showing the fire grate empty of garbage, her father's old duffel coat stuffed up the chimney, and twinkling reflections on the blank television screen. Darkness was bearable with the candle burning, and Sarah was reluctant to blow it out.

"Leave it," said Veronica. "Let's play cards."

"Oh, yes!" said William. "Strip-jack-naked!"

"And I want to play!" shouted Catherine.

"We don't have any cards," said Sarah.

Veronica produced a pack from her apron pocket. She had been through the front door and fetched them from the study. They sat on cushions on the dampened carpet and played until after midnight. Nobody argued. Nobody said anything hateful. Not even William when Catherine won. But William did grow tired and hungry. All he wanted, he said, was a dish of dog biscuits before he went to bed.

They did not have dog biscuits. They had a feast. Veronica sliced potatoes very thin into the frying pan, and when they were cooked she stirred in a pinch of dried herbs and four beaten eggs. Afterward they had cocoa made with powdered milk and two squares of chocolate each that Veronica had been hiding.

"That was yummy," said Catherine.

"Yummy Mommy! Yummy Mommy!" William chanted.

"How about cleaning your teeth?" Sarah suggested.

"We don't need to," said Catherine. "Because there aren't any dentists now and we won't ever have to go again."

"Which is all the more reason to clean your teeth," said Sarah. "Because if they go bad you'll have to have them pulled out with the pliers."

Catherine cleaned her teeth as she had never cleaned

them before, and William fell asleep in the chair with his clothes on. The stub of the candle guttered and died as Veronica strip washed over a bowl of cold water. Sarah lay in the darkness. She heard human sounds that no longer embarrassed her, Catherine's deep breathing, and the creak of the sofa as Veronica settled for the night.

"That was two extra candles and four eggs," said Sarah.

"I think we needed it," Veronica replied.

"Are you feeling better?"

"I'm sorry about today," Veronica said. "Sorry about yesterday too. I had no right to withdraw and leave you to cope. It was selfish, I see that now. Do you really think we can survive?"

"I think Catherine will," Sarah said confidently.

"Why Catherine?" Veronica asked.

"It's as if she knows," said Sarah. "As if she has an instinct. Right from the beginning she wouldn't drink that water, not even when I mixed it with milk powder. She had to have hers from the container. And she hardly comes out from under the table except to go to the toilet. She's managed to avoid contamination and she hasn't been exposed to the dust. I think we have to forget about ourselves and concentrate on her."

Veronica thought for a moment.

"If we die, how will she survive then?"

Sarah struggled to find the words.

"I don't know. I suppose we just have to trust. This is how things are meant to be and we're part of a plan. We don't need to see the reason and we can't question it, because the reason's out there, beyond us, with whatever it is that knows. We just do what we're supposed to do and make sure Catherine survives. All we are are fragments of some bigger meaning."

"You're talking about God," Veronica said quietly.

And maybe Sarah *was* talking about God.

For in the end people turned to Him.

ooo

Sarah sat up and listened. Something had woken her. And it came again . . . a rifle shot in the distance. She waited but heard nothing else. It was twenty past eight by her watch and she could have gone back to sleep, but instead she dressed and lit the candle. They had been wrong to put off starting the days, sleeping late and hoping it would soon be over. They needed to get back to a regular routine, the diurnal rhythm of waking and sleeping. Her body clock said it was morning, and her stomach said it was breakfast time. She allowed just enough milk powder to flavor the water and opened the last box of cereal. Then she set the kettle on the camping stove to boil and made her announcement.

"It's time to get up!"

"I'm up already," Catherine replied.

"What's the time?" Veronica muttered.

"Time to get up," Sarah repeated firmly.

She shook William awake. He was tired and irritable, refusing to wash his face when she told him to, refusing to eat shredded wheat. Shredded wheat was horrible, he said, and he wanted cornflakes. And when Veronica discovered it was only half past eight, she was irritable too. Sarah tried to explain. They needed to discipline themselves to avoid going crazy, and anyway she had heard shooting.

"And I did," said Catherine. "It was up on the hill at Harrowgate Farm. A person with a gun."

"Farmer Arkright's got a gun," William said darkly. "He showed it to me and Robert Spencer. He said he used it for shooting rabbits and little boys who trespass on his land. I didn't like him. He was horrible."

But it might not have been trespassers Farmer Arkright was shooting. It might have been something else. There were eggs, and chickens, and milk cows on Harrowgate Farm. If Farmer Arkright had shot a cow, he might give them meat, said Sarah. It would be contaminated, but they could still eat it and let Catherine have the cans.

"You're suggesting I should go there?" Veronica asked.

"We can't live on potatoes," said Sarah.

"I'll take the car," Veronica said.

"You could drive to the village and get me a chocolate bar," said William.

"I'd like my own little flashlight," Catherine said wistfully.

"The hardware store mightn't be looted," said Sarah. "We could do with more candles and another bottle of camping gas. And if we had some clear plastic wrap we could cover the kitchen window and expand our living quarters."

"Make a list," Veronica said.

They tore the flyleaf from the Bible, which was the only book Veronica had not thrown out. They listed everything they thought might be available . . . from

the drugstore, the hardware store, the village supermarket, and Harrowgate Farm. It was best to go now,
Sarah reasoned, while the dust was still falling and
people remained in their houses. If they waited until
the end of the two weeks, there would be nothing left.
There might be nothing left anyway, but it gave William something to dream about.

"Don't forget my cans of Coke and Crunchie bars!"
William shouted as Sarah closed the door and resealed
it with adhesive tape. "And don't forget my beefburgers and fish sticks, neither!"

Sarah listened to the rustle of Veronica's garbage-
bag steps across the kitchen floor, the rattle of the
safety chain, and Buster's soft miserable whine. Veronica talked to him sadly, words muffled by walls,
and a few minutes later they heard her drive away.

"I hope she remembers my beefburgers," William
said anxiously.

Sarah blew out the candle.

"There won't be any," Catherine stated. "You can't
have beefburgers without electricity."

"In the village there might *be* electricity," said
William.

"No there won't. There's no electricity anywhere."

"How do you know?"

"Because I'm in the junior school and you're only in
the infants'," Catherine said loftily.

"We could play school," Sarah suggested. "I could
be the teacher and you could be in my class. What's
four plus three, William?"

"You said we wouldn't have to go to school ever
again!" William said furiously. "And I don't want to
play school! I want to play cards like we did last night."

But last night's party was over and they could not recapture a time that was gone. They could only sit in the blind black dark waiting for Veronica to come home. And Sarah would not risk burning another extra candle. She did not share William's optimism that all the goods they had ordered would be delivered. "No!" said Sarah. And he flung the cards in her face.

Lunchtime came and Veronica had not returned. Sarah worried about violence and lawlessness, gangs of looters in a world gone mad. And there was nothing for lunch except potatoes boiled in their skins and a lump of dried cheese that Sarah made into sauce. William refused to eat it. The bookcase shelves were full of cans—meatballs, ravioli, sardines and tuna fish, salmon and luncheon meat—which William wanted instead, and Sarah would not give him.

"You can eat what's on your plate," she told him.

"Won't!" said William.

"I'll eat it," Catherine offered.

Sarah gave her William's potato.

"That's mine!" William howled.

It was a long wearying time without Veronica, having to cope with William alone. Sarah could feel her strength and patience being drained away. And when Veronica finally returned she was not alone. Sarah recognized the gruff tones of Farmer Arkright. She could not begin to imagine why he was there, but then, loud and deafening, just outside in the garden, came a single gunshot.

Buster died with a yelp, was buried in the cabbage patch . . . sounds of a shovel in dry earth. Human voices, woman and man, talked for a while and faded into silence. Catherine sobbed beneath the table. William got quiet, and slow tears trickled down Sarah's face. Then the car trunk slammed, and something rustled outside on the concrete like dry paper. She heard garden shears snipping through plastic wrap, listened as Veronica nailed it to the kitchen windowframe and sealed it with insulation tape. Then the lid of the rain barrel rattled and she went to work with the squeeze mop.

"I wonder if she's brought my Crunchie bar?" William said. He banged on the closed door, trying to gain Veronica's attention. "Have you got my Crunchie bar?" William shouted. Veronica ignored him, so he pushed against the door and broke the adhesive tape seal. His bare feet paddled through dust and soapsuds in the eerie half-light. "Have you got my Crunchie bar?" he repeated.

Veronica, when she turned to him, no longer looked like his mother. She looked more like a madwoman, old and haggard, with sunken eyes and matted unkempt hair. She had taken off her garbage-bag suit and her clothes were creased from where she had slept in them, her voice demented.

"Get back inside!" Veronica screamed. "And don't come out here again until I tell you! There weren't any Crunchie bars! I'm not a blasted magician!"

Sarah caught hold of William's arm and hauled him back into the room. He screamed and fought and struggled and hated. Then, in the depths of the armchair, he sat and cried . . . a five-year-old child, inconsolable in his disappointment, his expectations finally crushed. Soon, Sarah knew, he would cry for a different reason. Not for the loss of a Crunchie bar, but for water and bread.

∘∘∘

Veronica had not found much on her scavenging expedition. The shops had all been looted. But people at the church had given her two boxes of matches, a loaf of bread, and three boxes of soup. She had found several bars of diabetic chocolate and two dented cans of baby milk among the debris of the drugstore, and a few packets of potato chips and peanuts in the storeroom behind the bar. But Catherine had her flashlight, plus spare batteries, two packs of candles, and a cylinder of camping gas. Eggs and milk and meat had come from Harrowgate Farm, and a sack of low-grade potatoes for feeding livestock. The Spencers had gone from Brookside Cottage, Veronica said. She had searched the cupboards hoping to find food, but someone had been there before her, and no one was bothering about staying indoors.

"There's nothing left," Veronica said.

Dark light filtered through the plastic window, and Sarah gazed at the measly supplies spread along the freshly washed countertop. It was not enough to last them very long, and they were bound to eat the contaminated food, the milk and meat, leeks and cabbages, from the garden. Either from sickness or starvation they were certain to die. But William munched contentedly on a crust of bread and jam.

"What's in this box?" he asked.

"Nothing for us," Veronica said.

Sarah opened it. It was a gift for a world that would grow again, a world that she and William and Veronica would never see. Sarah stared at the packets of seeds—

peas, beans, onions and turnips, carrots and swedes, every vegetable imaginable. There and then they could have grown the cress seeds on the metal tea tray in a bed of newspaper, but she carefully replaced them and closed the lid. This box was for Catherine, an inheritance for life in a world where money was useless, and industry was gone.

The rest of the day was spent in the kitchen. There was just enough light to see by, a dreary perpetual twilight where the nuclear ash fell like snow over the outside land. Veronica never said how bad things really were, but Sarah could guess from her attitude, brooding and silent as she cooked the evening meal. It was a feast that would kill them . . . beefsteak, potatoes, and cabbage, with chocolate pudding for dessert. But it was easier to know and eat it than cling to the deprivation needed to survive. All Catherine ate was two cocktail sausages and a quarter of a can of baked beans. She ate it from a tray in her house under the table and would not come into the kitchen, not even to play cards.

Sarah peered through the gloom trying to distinguish hearts from diamonds, clubs from spades. There was no enjoyment, just a sense of duty, an obligation to keep William entertained. Growing cold and the evening darkness finally drove her inside, and all over again, after the comparative freshness of the kitchen, the stench of human excrement assailed her nostrils. Candlelight flickered and the door closed her in, and the long hard hours stretched all the way back to the morning. It was nine o'clock, but still William was not tired. Sarah played more card games, fed him cocoa and dog biscuits, and told stories from the Bible. He was asleep in the armchair by the time she reached Noah, but Catherine wanted her to tell more.

"And God looked on the earth and saw it was wicked, that men had corrupted his ways with their evil and violence, and he decided to destroy them with the earth."

"Is that what God's done now?" Catherine asked.

"He didn't make the bombs," said Sarah.

"But he knew we were wicked," said Catherine.

Maybe she was right, Sarah thought. Reports of evil and violence had appeared every day in the newspapers and on the television, and God had done nothing to stop them destroying themselves.

"When I grow up," Catherine said decisively, "I'm not going to be wicked. And I'm not going to let anyone else be wicked either. Then God won't have to do this again, will he?"

"It wasn't God's fault," Sarah said doubtfully.

"It wasn't ours either," Veronica said.

"I suppose it was the government," said Sarah. "But who elected them, Veronica? People like you and Daddy."

"And now we suffer for it," Veronica murmured.

"I'm not going to have a government when I grow up," said Catherine. "I'm going to live in the Garden of Eden, like Adam and Eve. Only there won't be any serpents because they've all died in the nuclear war."

Catherine could still dream. But Sarah had to face the reality, words out of darkness, Veronica telling her what it was like outside before she slept. People were not even trying to survive, Veronica said. It was like one big party, terrible, tragic, everyone congregated together in the church, and the chapel, and the

schoolrooms. Some of them were sick already, and
they were all half starved, yet they were willing to
share what they had. Farmer Arkright, Joe Sefton at
the bakery, the poultry farm on Winnow's Hill, were
delivering everything they could to the centers. As
the cows fell sick Farmer Arkright intended to shoot
them and butcher the carcasses. It was kinder that
way, Veronica said, and she had asked him to shoot
Buster out of kindness.

"But you can't shoot people," Veronica stated. "Not
even when you know they're going to die. We wouldn't
allow animals to suffer such a terrible death, yet we
expect it of people." She turned on the flashlight and
went to the sideboard drawer, brought out a bottle of
tablets and held them up to the light. "Just so you
know where they are when I'm gone," Veronica said.

Sarah nodded, watched her replace them. However
terrible living might become, she could not imagine
ever wanting to take them. In the beginning suicide
had been her suggestion, but now the roles were reversed. Veronica foresaw the time when death might
be preferable.

"I think we should face it now," Veronica said calmly.
"I don't want William to die, slowly and painfully, as
Buster would have done. He was bleeding from inside,
Sarah. There were sores around his eyes and his fur
was falling out. And I've seen those people at the
church. You have to promise me, Sarah. You have to
promise to look after William when I'm gone."

Her voice was pleading and the flashlight beam reflected in the darkness of her eyes, and at the corner
of her mouth was a small weeping sore. Something
cold and terrible landed in Sarah's stomach. That sore

was a symptom of radiation sickness and Veronica was already dying. That was why she thought of William and asked Sarah to promise. In the loneliness and silence Sarah reached for her hand, sweating and clammy and cold as ice. The precious person Veronica had become would soon be leaving her.

"I'll look after him, Veronica," she said.

And a lump rose to her throat as Veronica smiled.

ooo

Life was a little easier with the kitchen to move about in, more air, more space, and the gloomy natural light that came through the plastic window. Or maybe they had simply grown accustomed to their situation and become resigned. On the blue linoleum floor William played quietly with his Tonka truck, built houses out of Lego bricks or playing cards. Sometimes he even played with Catherine, Barbie doll games in her house beneath the table. Most of the time she still insisted on staying there, practicing her handwriting in Sarah's history exercise book by the light of her flashlight, reading about God and Noah and Adam and Eve, or sewing Barbie doll wedding dresses from the net curtains that had once hung at the kitchen windows. Catherine laughed and chattered like a normal little girl, but the rest of them had changed, as if something inside them were dying, their souls gone dull.

There was nothing to do, nothing to live for, or plan for, or talk about. They were gripped by an apathy from which they could not escape, without motivation, waiting to die, their body clockwork slowly winding down. They were not short of food. They had meat and milk and vegetables enough for several days, and enough cans to keep Catherine alive. And when it was gone Veronica went to Harrowgate Farm for more.

One by one as the cows fell sick, Farmer Arkright slaughtered them, shots heard at morning up on the hill. Daily in the Land Rover he delivered meat and milk to the village centers, and other farmers did the same. But the supplies were not limitless. Joe Sefton ran out of flour for making bread, and eggs got scarce at the poultry farm as more and more chickens died. Veronica said that starvation was no longer a worry, that human deaths were keeping pace with the deaths of the animals. They burned the bodies in the church-yard, the smoke of cremations adding to the darkness of the sky.

Sarah had no illusions. What was happening to Veronica would happen to herself and William. The sores spread on Veronica's face. Her gums bled. Her teeth came loose. And her hair came out in handfuls. And when the church bells rang, peal after peal of joyful clamorous sound telling them the two weeks were over, nothing changed. Their lives went on, day following day, with the dust still falling on the twilit land. No one advised them it was safe to go outside. There was no sound from the radio stations, and the days grew colder, and the sky at evening turned to the color of blood.

Sarah scrubbed clean the leeks Veronica had unearthed from the garden. Pale dust floated on the surface of the water, and William was plucking one of Farmer Arkright's chickens for a stew. He was not like the William they had always known. That lit-tle boy was gone. He had been outside and seen for

himself . . . a world of dust, rats and flies and putre-
fying bodies of sheep, Brookside Cottage empty and
abandoned, no one to play with and himself alone.
He was quiet and repressed, doing what he was told
without really caring, his blue eyes empty of life.

"If I could feel," Veronica said, "I think he would
break my heart."

Sarah knew what she meant. It was strange how
they simply stopped feeling, as if something inside
them turned off like a safety device. Nature was kind
after all. They were spared all the fear and panic,
hopelessness and horror, the inevitability of their deaths.
They simply accepted it, and quite dispassionately Sarah
could watch the spasm of pain that blanched Veronica's
ravaged face.

"Why don't you go and lie down?" she suggested.

But Veronica gripped her stomach.

And went outside.

It was maybe a month when the shooting stopped
at Harrowgate Farm and Veronica toiled up the hill
for the very last time. She was almost too sick to walk,
yet she insisted, and returned an hour later with a
dead maggoty chicken and a shopping bag full of canned
food. The Arkrights were dead, she said. She had found
them lying on the living-room floor, Farmer Arkright
and his wife, both shot in the head. She had covered
them with a sheet and rifled the pantry . . . canned
corned beef, sardines and pilchards, two cans of cat
food, and a bag of flour. She had not been able to carry
the bottled fruit, she said.

Sweating and shivering with fever, and clutching
her stomach, she went to lie down on the settee, and
Sarah sensed it was time for her to take over. She

dressed in the garbage-bag clothes, fetched the shopping cart from the garage, and told Veronica she was going. Whatever was left at Harrowgate Farm, they needed it.

It was Sarah's first sight of the world since the bombs had fallen . . . a chilling twilit world and a landscape of dust. Grass on the common was covered with gray, and the leaves on the larch trees were dying. There was a stink in the wind that cut cold across the common, a buzz of flies, and a rat scuttled from the open doorway of Brookside Cottage. Following Veronica's footsteps in the dust, Sarah dragged the shopping cart along the road, up the track through the farm fields, and into the cow yard. The stench was indescribable— blood and bones and the rotting remains of cattle, dung and sour milk and blocked-up drains. Rats attacked a sick cow chained in the milking barn, and somewhere a young calf cried.

Sarah gagged and held a handkerchief to her nose, her footsteps soundless in the dust as she went to investigate. Chickens lay dead among the outbuildings, and the storehouse roof had fallen in. She found the calves in a stone-built hay barn behind the tool shed—five of them, young and lively, with wide dark eyes. Farmer Arkright had made them a pen out of hay bales, and the arrow-slit windows were also stuffed with hay. Three metal troughs brimmed full of water, and bags of calf nuts lay open on the floor. Like Veronica's seeds they too were a gift for the future, the gift of a dead man to a child who would survive.

Sarah built a barricade before the hay-barn door. Tools and implements, piles of empty sacks, and wheelbarrows full of manure were tipped in a mound in front of it to prevent it being opened. The calves were for Catherine, and she had to protect her inheritance in any way she could. Sweating and stinking and filthy, Sarah worked until she was finally satisfied.

Then she went to the house, loaded the shopping cart with bottles of plums, gooseberries, strawberries, and apple pulp, and entered the boarded-up darkness of the living room. There was no need for her to go in there, Veronica had said, but she had found the box of cartridges on the kitchen table and she needed the gun. It was under the sheet, clutched in Farmer Arkright's hand. Dead fingers gripped and let go as Sarah pulled it free. She did not feel anything, neither revulsion nor pity. For Catherine's sake she would do what she had to, thieve from the living or the dead.

ooo

Sarah mashed potatoes with a can of Buster's dog food, made rissoles for dinner, and set them to fry. They would have bottled plums for dessert, she decided, or maybe not. They had had fruit every day since Sarah had visited the farm, and William was complaining of pains in his tummy. She opened a can of creamed rice pudding instead, spooned it into their unwashed breakfast dishes, and squirted chocolate sauce over the top.

Veronica came shuffling out to empty the commode, clung to the doors and walls for support, and made her way into the garden. Her teeth were broken and her head was a mass of oozing sores. Her eyes hurt in the light. A few hours ago she had vomited blood, but still she insisted on doing what she could; she rinsed the commode in the rain barrel and came back inside.

"William has diarrhea," she said.

"He's eaten too many plums," said Sarah.

"He's sick," said Veronica.

Sarah looked at her.

"I'll look after him," she said.

Maybe Veronica had needed to hear her say it one last time, for that night when William and Catherine were asleep she said she was leaving. She was just a burden, she said, and no more use. Dumbly in the candlelight Sarah watched her take some tablets from the bottle in the sideboard drawer. It was better this way, Veronica said. Better for all of them. And she was no longer afraid of death. It would be a relief. And the God Sarah believed in had no more plans for her.

Sarah nodded. This was the moment they had both faced up to long ago, and she did not try to stop her. It was not even terrible. The woman who had married her father had become in the end her only friend, and Sarah would never see her again. But the time was right and there was nothing left to say, not even good-bye. Maybe later she would cry and feel the grief, but now she simply accepted the end of Veronica, as soon, she would accept William's and her own. After so much suffering there could be no sadness in letting someone go.

"Will you be all right?" Sarah asked.

"I'll go to the church," Veronica said.

And closed the door.

It was the last Sarah saw of her, blue human eyes and a face covered with sores, turning to God. She snuffed out the candle and lay on her mattress on the floor. The room seemed empty now, a dark space where once Veronica had been. She could feel the loneliness like a pain. But by morning it had receded to a dull ache and Veronica was just a memory, a person who belonged to a green lost world and had nothing to do with now.

Mommy had gone for a walk, she told William and Catherine, and she did not know when she would be back. They asked no questions. Perhaps they too had gone beyond grieving or caring. They had dog-food rissoles for breakfast and William said his tummyache was better. But there were sores on his skin, and his eyes watered in the gloomy kitchen light. Death seemed to stare at Sarah from William's face, as if it were the only thing left in a world that had once been full of life. She wanted to do something, say something that would make him happy.

"Shall we go for a walk?" she suggested.

He shook his head.

"I don't like it outside," William said.

"And I have to stay and look after my Barbie doll," said Catherine.

"We might find some cans of food," said Sarah.

"I'm not hungry," said William.

Sarah gave him the gun. Veronica had managed to load it, and all William had to do was pull the trigger. He was to fire it, she said, if anyone came to the house. And she went out alone.

A chill wind blew across the darkened sky, whirled dead leaves from the trees and whipped up the dust, covered the tracks of shoes on the roadway. The wind that sang through the silence was the only sound, and Sarah shivered. Sores around her mouth cracked and bled, and small pains cramped her stomach. She had to find someone alive, someone for Catherine. But the houses around the common were blast damaged and empty, and from the village she could smell the death fires burning. Not in the church, or chapel, or schoolrooms would she find Catherine a home.

Sarah kept to the small lanes around the village outskirts, checking the isolated houses. They were all abandoned, and all she gained were a few cans of food. Dark wooded hills stretched out across the miles showing no light or life. And the July cold intensified as she headed back toward home.

A few drops of rain began to fall, pockmarks on the dust, as she went to Harrowgate Farm to check on the calves. The barricade was still there, blocking the haybarn door, and when she peered through a crack she saw the calves were alive, shadowy animals moving restlessly within the dark, warm womb of a future world, waiting for the child who would claim them, waiting for Catherine.

Rain swept across the barren land, black and icy, leaving its gritty traces on Sarah's face and hands. Pools of mud formed on the track, rivulets among the dust. Maybe the fields would grow again. Maybe it would wash the darkness from the skies. Pains gripped her stomach as she ran for shelter in Brookside Cottage, but it did not matter. She had only one thing left to do. She stole the baby carriage that had once belonged to Amanda Spencer, filled it with toys—Action men, Star Wars spaceships, battery-run robots, a sheriff's outfit and six-shooter gun . . . everything belonging to Robert that William had envied. He could play with them, Sarah thought. And perhaps he would be happy before he died.

◦◦◦

How long they had lived without Veronica Sarah did not know. Days passed quickly even though every minute seemed like an eternity of time. The sores on her face festered and spread. Like William she suffered from diarrhea and sickness, and not even Catherine could bear to live in the stinking vileness of the living room. Sarah rebuilt her house in the kitchen and removed the barricade from the living-room window. It let in the air and twilight and the gathering cold. Just for a few more days they lived like that, but then William vomited blood and she knew they must go.

She must take Catherine away. She did not know where but it had to be now, on the last morning, while she still had strength enough to travel. The baby carriage stood packed and ready and William lay on the settee, wrapped in blankets and shivering with fever, too ill to move. His eyelids were swollen and weeping, his golden hair fallen and gone. Sarah knelt beside him, feeling the heat of his forehead beneath her hand.

"Catherine and I are going for a walk," she said.

William nodded, not really caring.

"We might be gone for a long time," Sarah went on. "All day, perhaps. You'll have to stay here, William. I've opened a can of pineapple chunks. They're here on the floor, right where you can reach them. Do you understand?"

"Will you come back?" William asked feebly.

"Just as soon as I can," Sarah promised.

Catherine stood in the doorway, unrecognizable in the torn garbage-bag suit. She had a handkerchief tied over her nose and mouth and a plastic bag with airholes over the top. She did not yet know that somewhere out in the dark desolate world Sarah would abandon her.

"You can pull the shopping cart," Sarah told her.

"Where are we going?" she asked.

"We'll know when we get there," said Sarah.

She turned the baby carriage and heaved it through the doorway. Saucepans, dangling from the sides, rattled and banged. There were shoes and slippers and Wellington boots on the rack underneath, and the seeds and shotgun and cans of food were hidden inside, beneath the jumble of Catherine's clothes. Blankets and a sleeping bag were piled on top and covered with plastic wrap torn from the kitchen window. Nothing showed of any value except for the half-empty bag of dog biscuits.

"And that's all we've got if anyone asks," she told Catherine. "Just dog biscuits. Remember that."

"Are we going to look for Mommy?" Catherine asked.

"No," said Sarah. "We're going to look for somewhere better to live."

Dragging the shopping cart, Catherine followed behind. It was loaded with bottles of fruit that clinked in the silences, with a nightgown, sponge bag, and Barbie doll riding on top. Wheels made tracks in the sodden dust and a damp wind blew in their faces. The sky grew darker, an eerie gloom that swallowed the shapes of trees and houses, a wintery cold that chilled them to the bone. They were heading into it, a freezing journey that had no foreseeable end.

"I'm cold," said Catherine. "I want to go home."

"We'll go home afterward," said Sarah.

She hoped they would not meet any people, but there was no one alive on this side of the village so they had to go past the church. There was a fire in the graveyard with dark shapes moving around it, and someone leaning on the lych gate watching them approach, a man coming toward them through the morning darkness and a woman following behind. It was the first fear Sarah had felt since the bombs had fallen.

"What's in that carriage?" the man asked.

"Things," said Sarah. "We're looking for somewhere to live."

"Food!" said the man.

"No," said Sarah.

"Only dog biscuits," Catherine said fearfully.

The woman shuffled forward.

"I know you, don't I? It's Sarah, isn't it? Sarah Harnden from across the common. You know Sarah, Ted? Veronica's daughter. She came to us the other night."

"Dead," said the man. "Veronica's dead."

"And I'm Mrs. Porter," said the woman.

Sarah remembered Mrs. Porter. She had been fat once, but now she was thin, bald and shivering in the wind, dying as Sarah was. Catherine was crying because the man had said Veronica was dead, and Mrs. Porter wanted them both to come into the church, where everyone else was living. But Sarah had to get away from them. She had to take Catherine away.

"I'll wheel the carriage," said the man.

"You don't understand!" Sarah said desperately. "My sister isn't sick! She's not sick at all! I have to find somewhere for her to live, a person, a place. She can't stay with us!"

Mrs. Porter stared at Catherine's hidden face.

"I think we should let them go," she told the man.

"They've got food!" he insisted.

"Didn't you hear what she said? The child isn't sick. That food is for her." Mrs. Porter turned to Sarah. "You go, my dear. You take your sister away. Ted won't stop you. He's not a bad man."

Ted spat on the road as Sarah passed.

"*He* won't help you!" he said bitterly. "He'll turn you away, same as he turned us away. And all he'll give you is lettuce!"

The saucepans jangled, and the fruit bottles clinked in the shopping cart as Sarah and Catherine walked away along the street of abandoned houses. The fire in the churchyard faded behind them and the man's words echoed in Sarah's head. *He* would not help them, the man had said, and all he would give them was lettuce. Whom had he meant?

"I don't want to go!" wept Catherine. "I don't want to go and live with that horrible man! Don't make me go, Sarah! I want to stay with you and William!"

Johnson, thought Sarah. It had to be Johnson. She remembered going there last summer with her father, driving along a track through the woods. His place was a forestry lodge that had been converted to a smallholding, fields growing hay grass and string beans, and a dozen glass houses. She remembered seeing goats in a paddock and a stream with a sheep-dip not far away. They had bought two boxes of pansies from a bearded man who had said his name was Johnson, and stayed to talk. He said he had moved there from London five years ago. Opted out of the rat race, he said. It was miles from anywhere, and his wife had left him, and he had sold his produce at the local market. There were no utilities, just an electric generator and septic-tank drainage, and his water was pumped from an underground well. Veronica had said she was not surprised his wife had left him, living in such primitive isolated conditions.

"He shouted at me!" sobbed Catherine. "He shouted rude words and told us to go away! All we did was swing on his gate! We never meant to let the sheep in his field! I don't like him, Sarah!"

"You'll like him this time," Sarah said.

Spasms of pain racked her body as she pushed the baby carriage down the long road past Ryelands Guest House and up the hill toward the next village. Sleet lashed her face and the dark woods waited, and there were two miles to go before they came to a turning on the right. And although Catherine cried, Sarah could smile. This was how things were meant to be and Johnson was part of the plan.

◦◦◦

Once off the road it was hard walking. The carriage jolted over loose stones, and the shopping cart leaked crimson juice from a broken bottle of plums. Fallen trees and broken branches blocked the track and they had to detour through mounds of dusty undergrowth. Sarah was weak and sweating with the effort, and twice she had to stop to be sick. Then from the high empty hilltop where the trees had been felled, she saw the smallholding below, glass houses bright with electric light and pale smoke rising from the cottage chimney.

"I don't want to go there," Catherine said bleakly.

SARAH /59

"I know," said Sarah. "But there's nothing else I can do. And he'll look after you, you see."

Johnson came to meet them at the bottom of the track, the shape of a man in a navy-blue overall, lean and tall in the twilight. An improvised helmet with a curved plastic visor concealed his face and he carried a shotgun. He had survived like Catherine because he took no chances, and the shotgun was aimed at Sarah's head.

"I don't want to hurt you," Johnson said quietly. "But I'll kill you if I have to. I can give you lettuce. Take it and go."

Sarah pushed Catherine toward him.

"I'll go," she said. "But I'll leave Catherine here. We've taken good care of her. She isn't sick and she's able to work for her keep."

Johnson stared and hesitated.

Then lowered the gun.

"I've been waiting for this," he said.

"You'll take her?" Sarah asked.

"I'm not much good with kids," said Johnson. "Never had any of my own, but I'll take her. What did you say her name was?"

"Catherine," said Sarah.

Johnson nodded and opened the gate.

"Bring your shopping cart, little lady."

Alone, without Sarah, Catherine crossed the threshold of Johnson's land and stood forlornly beside him. Live chickens scratched in a nearby glass house, and there were goats and sheep in another. Others contained lettuce, and cucumbers, and unripe tomatoes, trays of seedlings, and bedding flowers. The blast had not damaged them. The glass was plastic and the hills formed a sheltering amphitheater all around. It was a good place in which to survive. Sarah parked the carriage against the dry stone wall.

"You'd better have Catherine's things," she said. "There's seeds too, and all the canned food we had left, and a twelve-bore shotgun."

"A gun," said Johnson. "You've got a gun?"

"One like yours," said Sarah.

Johnson laughed.

"This gun's not real," he said. "It only works by fooling people. I carved it out of wood the week after the bombs went off, and painted it to look like real. Real enough to frighten people away, anyhow."

"They told us in the village you would turn us away," Sarah informed him.

Johnson sighed.

"What else could I do? I had to turn those poor devils away. I don't have enough food to feed the whole wretched population. Enough for the living maybe, but not for the dying. If food would have saved them I would have given it willingly, believe me."

Sarah did believe him.

"Will you come and stay with your sister?" he asked.

Sarah shook her head.

"I have to go home," she said. "My little brother is sick. I see you have outbuildings here. There are five live calves at Harrowgate Farm waiting to be collected. Nobody knows they're there. I barricaded the barn door to keep them safe, but I think you should have them. You can use Farmer Arkright's Land Rover, and there's diesel in a tank by the toolshed."

A squall of icy rain came sweeping down from the hills, ran like tears down Johnson's covered face as he lifted his eyes to the sky. He said if he had never believed in God before, he believed in Him now. And this was the beginning of a brave new world. Sarah shivered and pulled up the hood of her duffel coat. She had to go, she said, and looked at the garbage-bag figure of Catherine for the last time. Johnson rested his hand on the child's shoulder.

"I'll look after her," he said. "I'll teach her to grow. We'll build a world from the dust, she and I. It won't be easy, but we'll do it. A society based on human decency, free people, cooperating without violence, better than the old. There's a nuclear winter coming on, cold like we have never known. But the glass houses are centrally heated. There's plenty of wood. The well water's good. If I can get diesel enough to keep the generator going . . . if I can scavenge enough hay and concentrates to keep the animals alive . . . if I can keep the green plants growing . . . we'll make it, your sister and I."

Sarah coughed and smiled. Bright blood flecked the back of her hand and she did not worry. Johnson was part of the plan, a man with a vision that she herself would never share. Her part was over, her purpose played out. She had lived for Catherine and now she gave Catherine to him. Finally satisfied, Sarah turned away, leaving man and child together in the rainy darkness.

"I'll call you Kate," she heard him say. "And you call me Johnson. There will be others, I expect, but it's you and I who have to make ready."

Johnson and Catherine, the baby carriage and the shopping cart, went rattling away toward the house as Sarah headed home up the long track. She had no reason now to go on living. Death would be a relief, Veronica had said, and in the sideboard drawer the bottle of tablets waited. She would give half to William and take the rest herself, two lives ceasing together. It was better that way.

Pains gripped her stomach and she vomited blood, and the hood of her duffel coat rubbed raw the sores on her scalp. In a world that was dark and ugly, where the wind whined through the silences, Sarah knew that she was ugly too—her youth and prettiness, her love and life and hope, laid waste by the holocaust of war. But some things could never be destroyed: a child with her dreams . . . a man with his visions . . . and a gorse flower that bloomed in the dust. Sarah touched it, damp yellow petals, gold and fragile and strong. Alive and beautiful, it bloomed for the future, radiated the glory of God. In the end people turned to Him, and Sarah could not be sorry.

PART TWO

OPHELIA

Quite by chance Bill Harnden survived the nuclear war. Normally he would have been lecturing at Bristol University, but that afternoon he had had to drive to Bath for a meeting of the South West Arts Committee. Suddenly a woman came running from a wayside cottage and flagged him down. She told him her name was Erica Kowlanski and she was a leading authority in the cellular cloning of vegetable and animal protein. She showed him a blue identity card that guaranteed her a place in any nuclear fallout shelter, and begged him to drive her there.

Bill had been fully aware of the dangerous international situation, but that was the first he had heard of the imminence of a nuclear attack. It was the car radio, not Erica Kowlanski, that finally convinced him it was really happening. His first instinct was to turn the car around and head for home. But home was thirty miles away across the river Severn, and London had already been hit. With Bristol next on the strike list, he knew he would never make it. All he had time for was to save the woman and himself.

"My pass will cover both of us," she said urgently.

Shocked out of thinking, Bill Harnden followed her directions, drove along byroads east of Bath. The road led uphill, toward wooded escarpment, and he could see the streets of Georgian houses below and traffic snarl-ups along the highways, and hear the sirens of police cars wailing. Then the road dipped down and quiet fields took over, England on a sleepy afternoon in early summer, full of bluebells and buttercups and cattle grazing. He could not believe it was all about to end.

"Turn left at the next junction," Erica Kowlanski said.

High wire fences and red notice boards told him that the area ahead belonged to the Ministry of Defense, and wire gates guarded the entrance to a disused stone quarry. Soldiers checked the woman's pass and waved Bill through. He parked among armored cars and black official limousines, transferred to an army truck full of civic dignitaries and top civil servants, and was driven away.

A concrete tunnel and a roadway of curving light led deep inside the hill. Corridors branched away in all directions like blood vessels from a heart. He stood and waited in a great reception hall, a lone civilian among all the military personnel. It was more than a bunker. It was a vast purpose-built subterranean city, a labyrinth of rooms and passageways, as if the whole hill had been hollowed out. It was not the only one, Erica Kowlanski informed him. Scattered over England there were maybe a dozen underground complexes such as this. He guessed he could count himself lucky as the outer doors closed and sealed him inside.

Or was it luck, Bill thought, to be separated from his wife and children, to know that they died while he lived on? Alone in his cell room shared with a couple of American G.I.s, sitting on a hard bunk bed and staring at the blank pale-green walls around him, somehow he could not think of it as luck. Apart from his briefcase containing lecture notes, a volume of *Hamlet* that Veronica had given him for Christmas, and a photograph of her and the children that he kept in his wallet, he had brought nothing with him to remind him of his former life. He was a man in a vacuum, and everything he loved was swept away.

Time, of course, healed his grief. He grew used to the regimented routine of the bunker, mealtimes and work shifts, days and nights that began and ended with the sound of a buzzer. He grew used to the communal living of dining halls, assembly halls, shower and relaxation rooms, Grant and Elmer who shared his cell, and the total lack of privacy. A degree in English literature was useless there, and so was he. He was put to work in the supplies department, shifting dehydrated foodstuffs from the storerooms to the canteen kitchen, a man in a navy-blue government-issued overall, number 423 on the admissions list, his identity gone.

Among all the high-ranking army and air-force personnel, among all the lords mayor, county surveyors, education and police chiefs, top scientists, communications experts, district administrators, and Americans from the nearby airbase, Bill was just a low-status civilian at the bottom rung of the hierarchy. He did what he was told and was not expected to question it, nor did he know what went on among the upper echelons of power.

General MacAllister, who was in charge of the Avon Bunker, was not a man to be found mixing socially with his subordinates. A remote mustachioed figure in a khaki uniform, he issued the orders, but he did not confide. All Bill knew of the overall situation was what filtered down to him through the ranks. As Elmer so succinctly put it, the contingency plans for surviving nuclear war had been one almighty screw-up.

The Avon Bunker had been constructed to house seven hundred and fifty people, with supplies for up to two years. In actual fact less than five hundred of those who had been designated places actually reached it in time. Due to radioactive fallout, communication with other bunkers was impossible to establish, nor, at the end of the statutory fourteen days, could they begin to administer law and order and emergency aid to the surviving population of the Bath-Bristol region. It was more than six weeks before the radiation level dropped below critical. By that time there was apparently no civilian population left alive. The cities were flattened, and the nuclear winter had set in.

Temperatures plummeted way below zero. England became as cold as Siberia and the dust remained in the upper atmosphere, obscuring the sun. Snow lay twenty feet thick, covering the ruins of cities in a white, freezing shroud. There could be no reconnoitering, no aerial surveys to assess the final damage.

Radio communication still remained difficult, but it seemed that three major bunkers, at Plymouth, Cheltenham, and Cardiff, had not survived. Those surviving in the minor bunkers were cut off, some buried beneath the rubble of buildings, some short of supplies. But the blizzards raged. Hurricane-force winds had been recorded. And Avon could not assist.

Stocked to minister to the requirements of the whole Bristol-Bath catchment area, the Avon Bunker had no shortage of food or clothing or medical supplies. But the prefabricated field hospitals, tent shelters for the homeless, and mobile soup kitchens were never used. The prewar estimates for survival had been proved wrong. For those outside, the chance of survival was next to nothing, and those in the bunker were there for life. Bill Harnden would never be going home.

ooo

The nuclear winter lasted for almost two years. Not until the sunlight returned and the long darkness ended could the government bunkers begin to collate their evidence. From Cambridge, Cumbria, Avon, Rosyth, Hereford, Derby, and Yorkshire, the helicopters made their surveys. Incredibly, people *had* survived outside, but the population of the British Isles—which, before the war, had been an estimated sixty-five million—had been reduced to a handful . . . tiny scattered settlements of people struggling to survive in the desolate wastes of a once-productive land. And for them it was only the beginning. Sickness, starvation, mutation, and radiation-linked cancers would reduce them still further over the years to come.

Nothing grew in the cold, black deserts of nuclear dust. But the slow sun warmed the land, and in a few more months, the scientists predicted, it would begin to grow. Then it was discovered that the ozone layer around the earth had been damaged by the holocaust, and too much ultraviolet light was passing through the atmosphere. This would cause skin burns, skin cancer, retinal damage to the eyes, and congenital deformity. Protective clothing had to be worn by anyone venturing outside, and it seemed that human beings would never again freely inhabit the surface of the earth.

Bill Harnden continued his life in the Avon Bunker, but he was not entirely happy with the situation. Military men with no one left to conquer, administrators with no population to administrate, civic dignitaries, civil servants, and police chiefs were all professionally useless, no different from himself. Yet they continued to cling to the ranks the world had once bestowed on them, and expected him to obey. They seemed to think that they, like the children of Israel, were the chosen few . . . destined to rule over a kingdom that would soon recover. A Union Jack flag fluttered, red, white, and blue, a symbol of triumph on the top of an empty hill. It did not occur to them that Britain, like the rest of the civilized world, had been defeated.

"It is our duty," General MacAllister said, "to restore this country to what it was."

He actually believed it could happen, that the mines would reopen, the factories would be rebuilt, and industry would start again. Planning committees were formed. New contingency plans were drawn up and submitted to central government in the Berkshire

Bunker, and their own bunker extended outward. Bill was transferred from stores to manual labor. Along with Grant and Elmer, supervised by an American army colonel by the name of Jeff Allison, and dressed in white protective suiting, he helped to clear the surrounding land of its sterile surface of dust. The prefabricated field units were put into use, bolted to metal girders, and the whole area roofed over with sheets of transparent corrugated plastic to form a vast glass house. They grew fresh vegetables and cereal crops, and Erica Kowlanski went to work in the food-processing laboratory.

The first batch of cloned root vegetables was harvested eight weeks later, and army personnel with government requisition orders scoured the surrounding countryside for any animals that might have survived. Half a dozen sheep, a few dozen chickens, and three goats were brought to the bunker from a settlement in the Cotswold Hills, legalized theft that formed the basis of a breeding flock. Eggs were cloned. But the fertilized chicken embryos all showed signs of mutation, and new grass planted in the outside fields seared brown in the sun. They lacked the means for successfully raising livestock, and women, who had not rated very high on the government's list of priority survivors, suddenly assumed a significance.

Excluding a few elderly wives and growing daughters, there were only thirty-two women in the whole bunker who were capable of conceiving and giving birth to children, and Erica Kowlanski was one of them. Bill never really knew why she sought him out. It had nothing to do with love and little to do with affection. She admitted, quite freely, that she had never wanted marriage or children, that she found the idea abhorrent. But now she saw it as a necessary duty, and she was not the kind of woman to turn her back. Bill understood. She was not offering to be a wife to him in the way Veronica had been. She had simply chosen him to father her child. And one year later, after a long and difficult labor, Erica gave birth to a baby girl.

Erica was forty-one years old and Bill was almost fifty. And even if it was her duty, Erica swore she would never go through it again. She was a woman devoid of all maternal instincts, and maybe that was why she had chosen Bill for a mate. She had sensed perhaps that he would make up for her inadequacy, that he had fathered before and would love the child enough for both of them.

Under the white-hot lights of the hospital ward Bill took his daughter in his arms. She did not remind him of William or Catherine. She reminded him of Sarah, and a marriage gone wrong. Marriage to Erica was wrong too, but he could not regret this child. She would make up for the children he had lost, and he could not love her more.

In the next bed to Erica, Jeff Allison's wife cradled her second Anglo-American son. Wayne Jeffrey, like his brother Dwight, had been conceived out of love, not duty. Next time, Mrs. Allison vowed, she too would have a girl. But Bill smiled down at his own little daughter and knew he would never have another. The small face puckered to cry, and Erica handed him the feeding bottle.

"What will you call her?" Mrs. Allison asked.

"Ophelia," said Bill. "And let her not walk i' the sun."

ᴏ–ᴏ–ᴏ

Ophelia assumed she would never walk in the sun. For
her the sun was a dim yellow disc seen through the
plastic roof of the cultivation area, an m-type star ninety-
three million miles distant. It shone on the great solar
panels on the hilltop above her and indirectly provided
her with warmth and light, charging the battery cells
that worked the electric generator on which life in the
bunker depended.

She was not unhappy in her little regimented world
of rooms and passageways. She had been born and
brought up there and knew nothing different. In the
schoolrooms, her father taught what life had been like
before the holocaust, but to Ophelia it did not seem
relevant. And although she loved the rich language of
English literature—sceptred isles set in silver seas
and season of mists and mellow fruitfulness—it was
all remote and unreal, as unreal as the images seen in
dreams and instantly forgotten. It was ancient history.
Western civilization, like the Greek and Roman em-
pires, was irretrievably gone. Only the memory was
kept alive, the ambition to rebuild it that General
MacAllister conceived as a duty and Dwight Allison
said was futile.

Ophelia did not much care who was right or wrong.
She saw only what was actual, an outside world that
was treeless and hostile, a landscape eroded by wind
and rain and sun. Telescreens showed it in the main
communications room, outside cameras panning the
rock-strewn deserts of Avon and Gloucestershire,
Wiltshire and Somerset. Rain had washed away the

surface soil. Snow and frost and fog of winter gave way in summer to bleak baked hills and barren valleys where nothing much grew . . . just tussocks of brittle grass, a few hardy flowers, and pockets of vegetation along the river margins. Packs of scavenging dogs hunted the tiny nomadic herds of sheep and goats that roamed the plains, and red pins on a map of England showed the scattered communities of human survivors. It was bad land around the bunker, and the ultraviolet light was too intense for agriculture.

Down in the valley by the river, conditions were a little better. Men in white protective suits planted wheat and potatoes in fields of dung and dust, and reaped a small annual harvest. But the conifers had shriveled on the hillside and the few surviving sheep were horribly deformed. Most of them were blind. Some had stumps instead of limbs and gave birth to lambs with multiple heads and twisted spines, and chickens were hatched in the laboratory incubators with white, pupilless eyes. The white-eyed gene was a dominant mutation, Dr. Stevenson said. Even rats were affected, and the only things that thrived in the land outside were lizards and flies.

Mostly the northern hemisphere could not support much life. Years before, the aerial surveys had shown the continents laid waste, from the Baltic Sea to the Mediterranean, across industrial Europe and the United States of America—a world gone dead. Now the supplies of gasoline and diesel had almost run out, and no one knew if anything had changed among the small settlements of human survivors.

Inside the bunker nothing ever changed. It was a constant environment, just as Ophelia had always known

it. Maybe, as Dwight said, it got a little crummier with
every day that passed, but it was hardly noticeable—
except when the electric generator broke down and
had to be repaired. And although the concrete structure was cracked and crumbling in places, the videos
and computers went on working, and Ophelia assumed
they would go on working forever.

Clone vegetables grew in the culture tanks in Erica's
laboratory. Edible protein was culled from blue-green
algae, and extract of sugar beet provided sweetness.
Food plants flourished in the cultivation area where
the sunlight filtered through the plastic roof and the
rain rattled. Ophelia liked to go there, walk among the
smells of damp earth and green things growing, among
the splashed colors of ripe red tomatoes and yellow
squash flowers.

Sometimes, after watching a video film or visiting
the cultivation area, she could almost envision the lost
world her father talked of. But she could not imagine
the taste of chocolate biscuits, the smell of beefsteak
braised in wine, or the song of the blackbird. Bill Harnden could not convey taste, and scent, and sound, to
someone brought up in concrete corridors, on cloned
eggs and carrot juice, where human voices were the
only natural sounds. He could not convey past realities
in a windowless classroom to these children of the dust.

Without textbooks or writing materials he tried to
teach them literature and history. With only computer
video pictures he tried to teach them art. Lacking the
basic tools for making things, he tried to teach them
crafts. He insisted they needed a fully comprehensive
education, that concentration on math and science and
computer learning did not make for a balanced intel-

lect. He believed that a teacher was more than an educational supervisor, that human interactions were of paramount importance to understanding, that the stimulation of a child's imagination was even more necessary than teaching it to calculate. On those issues he clashed with the bunker hierarchy, with the education chief, with General MacAllister, and with his wife.

"We need creative thinkers," said Bill. "Not a generation of automatons!"

"Logical thought can be just as creative," Erica said.

"It's a dead end without imagination. The human brain has two sides to it and both are meant to be used. What's the good of raising calculative geniuses who are incapable of understanding anything but their own calculations? One-track minds, blind to all else?"

In the small family apartment with pale-green walls, where the paint flaked away to show bare plaster underneath, Ophelia listened as her parents exchanged words. Usually, in the evenings, there was only herself and her father, with Erica working away in the laboratory, but tonight she had joined them. The conversation that had begun in the dining hall over a meal of chicken-flavored soybean stew still continued. Apparently Mrs. Allison was having trouble with Dwight, and Erica blamed Bill. She said his unconfined teaching methods were filling his head full of stuff and nonsense and rebellious ideas.

"These young people have to accept things as they are," Erica said. "They don't need to know how things used to be, or what things might become again in the future. We don't need dreamers. We need scientists and technologists. They're the ones who will make the

breakthrough, Bill. They're the ones on whom our
future depends."

"You're darned right!" said Bill. "Our future *does*
depend on them . . . their ability to create something
better than the world we have now, or the world of
the past. If they don't know about the past, they have
nothing to compare the present to, and nothing to feed
their imaginations on which a future society depends."

"That imagination has to be fostered in the right
way!" Erica retorted. "You're encouraging them to
want what they can't have! Flipping poetics, Bill!
Beauty, and truth, and freedom, the pursuit of personal happiness . . . there's no room for that in an en-
closed environment. Dwight Allison is a very clever
boy. We need his skills. If we can't get a breakthrough
in genetic engineering, then we'll have to go on living
underground. He could design the city of the future . . . a brilliant architect, Bill, if you don't turn
him into a blasted revolutionary!"

"What use is an architect who can't make bricks?"
Bill asked her. "We're teaching all the wrong things!
If we forget how to use our hands and our hearts, what
good can we do with our heads? Who's going to build
the fabled city?"

"When the time comes, we'll recruit outside work-
ers," Erica said.

"Suppose they don't want to be recruited?"

"Oh, come on, Bill! Everyone has to work for a
living."

"They *are* working, woman! They're working for
themselves! Working to survive in conditions like we
have never known! What right do we have to expect
them to give up their own enterprises and work for

us? It's you who are the dreamer, Erica! You, and the rest of the make-Britain-great-again brigade. This place will fall down around our ears while you're still sitting on your butt hoping for a scientific breakthrough. It's not going to happen—and Dwight sees that."

Ophelia chewed her fingernails. Her parents quarreled. They seldom did anything else but quarrel. They were not like Dwight's parents, loving each other and him. Harsh light shone on the green linoleum floor, shone on her father's gray hair and Erica's glasses. There was a flush on her face, and her eyes flashed with annoyance, and she was not about to give up.

"Without technology you wouldn't be alive now!" Erica said furiously.

"And countless millions of people wouldn't be dead!" retorted Bill. "Lest we forget: It was science and technology that invented the bomb and devastated the earth . . . not to mention blokes like MacAllister with his blind obedience to central government policy. Is that what you call creative thinking, Erica?"

Erica put on her white laboratory overalls.

"I'm going!" she said.

"Maybe one day you'll face it!" said Bill.

There was a knock on the door.

And Erica opened it.

"Domestic harmony is one beautiful thing," said Colonel Allison in his slow American drawl. "You can hear it all the way to the recreation room."

"What do you want?" Erica asked sourly.

"Ophelia," said Colonel Allison. "A message from Dwight. There's baseball in the storage depot, and you're to report to second base."

"And stop biting your nails!" said her father.

⌀○⌀

There were one hundred and twenty-two children in
the Avon Bunker, their ages ranging from Mrs. Sut-
cliffe's two-month-old baby to Dwight Allison, who
was seventeen. There was a day-care center and kin-
dergarten for the little ones and graded education for
the rest. Schooling began at 0900 hours and ended at
1700 hours, and included supervised sports sessions
with Sergeant Major Wilkinson in the recreation hall.
With so many experts in the bunker they did not lack
qualified tuition. At sixteen Ophelia was already
studying advanced genetics with Dr. Stevenson two
afternoons a week. She knew how to dissect the ovum
of a rat and isolate the gene that gave rise to muta-
tional blindness. She could remove and replace it with
a nonmutated chromosome from a bunker-bred rat.
But in the next generation the mutation recurred if
the rats were exposed to outside ultraviolet light. In
cartography Bernard Sowerby was updating ordi-
nance survey maps from aerial photographs, and Dwight
was working on designs for an elevator shaft to a pro-
jected lower basement area.

Educationally they were far in advance of prewar
standards, yet they were still considered children. They
still played baseball in the storage depot, collected
cockroaches and raced them along the dining-hall tables, fed invasion messages from outer space into the
main computer, and got rips in the navy-blue government-issued overalls. They were still, during weekends and evenings, part of the noisy unruly horde of
youngsters who careered through the confines of the

bunker, believing it unconditionally theirs. But once too often some unidentified child robbed the cultivation area of its ripe tomatoes. And once too often some unidentified child visited the communications room, overheard communiqués from central government, and blabbed restricted information. A rumor spread that the prime minister was dead and Air Marshal Hughes had taken over. Bill Harnden discussed it during a schoolroom debate.

"Is this the end of democracy?" he asked.

"What democracy?" said Dwight. "Avon has been a totalitarian state for the last twenty years."

Ophelia was not much interested in politics. The bunker had always been run by General MacAllister, and it made no difference to her who governed the rest of the country. It was General MacAllister who imposed the restrictions, placed the cultivation area and the communications room out of bounds to all persons under the age of eighteen. She missed the feel of sunlight through plastic, the smells of warmth and dampness and green things growing. She missed the blue of the sky and the gray-black deserts seen on the telescreens. Her concrete world seemed shrunken in size.

Now her only visual stimuli were the pale-green walls of the bunker, the geometrical perspectives of rooms and corridors, human faces, and the schoolroom computer screens. Something of freedom had been taken away and she experienced a feeling of loss. But it never occurred to her to question it. She had been brought up to respect the routine and the discipline, the restrictions imposed on her life. For the good of all people she was prepared to accept a personal loss, but there were other young people who were not so willing.

They met in the storage depot, most of Bill Harnden's senior-grade pupils who usually played in the baseball match. White paint on the concrete floor marked out their field, but that evening was different. Younger children played in the defunct cold-storage units, or clambered about the broken army vehicles parked at the far end. But the older ones huddled together, seated on prewar packing cases in a dimly lit corner of the room. Rusting paint cans were piled against a nearby wall and their voices echoed, angry and indignant.

"MacAllister's got no right!" Dwight said bitterly.

"You mean *we've* got no rights," said Bernard Sowerby.

"Nobody has," said his sister. "Nobody has any real say in how this bunker is run."

"I even heard Pop say he was sick of following orders," Wayne Allison said.

"But he still goes on doing it!" Dwight said angrily.

"He's got no choice," said Gaynor.

"Nor has MacAllister," said Spotty Harris. "He gets his orders from central government."

"It's not central government who's banned us from going into the communications room!" Dwight said furiously. "It's that pig MacAllister! The man's a military dictator! He wasn't voted into office, so what right does he have to rule us?"

"What does it matter who rules us?" Ophelia remarked.

Dwight rounded on her.

"If it doesn't," he said, "then it damned well ought to! Your father's spent the last five years trying to tell us! It's the right, and duty, and responsibility, of every individual to question everyone and anyone who assumes authority over us! If those millions of people had gotten off their backsides and questioned what they all knew was going on, maybe they wouldn't be dead, and we wouldn't be stuck in this crummy bunker! No one should have power over other people. Your father has told us what governments and men like MacAllister can do! They destroy not only people's lives but the whole damned world! And if you don't know that, Ophelia, you must be stupid!"

Ophelia stared at him. She had known Dwight Allison all her life and he had never once spoken to her like that. Tears pricked the backs of her eyes as she turned and walked away. Silence followed her across the cold concrete spaces. She heard an army truck back from its sortie come rumbling along the main tunnel. Young children giggled in the cold-storage unit, and the intercom crackled ordering Police Chief James to report to administration. Ophelia pushed open the closed double doors and entered the corridor. Footsteps came running behind. There were strip lights missing from the ceiling, making areas of gloom, and she thought it was Dwight. But it was Wayne, his brother, who fell into step.

"Dwight didn't mean it," he said.

"So why did he say it?" Ophelia asked.

"Mom says it's the age he's at."

"You're only one year younger than he is! And you didn't call me stupid!"

"He's lousy to everyone," said Wayne.

Men from the army truck came whistling along the corridor. They wore white suits with clear plastic visors that made them eyeless in the light. They talked of finding gasoline at Milford Haven, thousands of gallons in an untapped storage tank, enough to send the helicopter out on an aerial survey, airborne again after seven years.

"Did you hear what they said?" Wayne asked excitedly.

Ophelia leaned against the wall. She did not care about the helicopter or what it might find. She only cared about Dwight, sixteen years of friendship coming to an end because he was having trouble growing up. Ophelia was growing up too, but she had not let it spoil things. And it was not just hormones causing Dwight to change his attitude toward her, it was her father's teachings!

○○○

Ophelia was not present when Dwight found the spray can and wrote the message on the wall—GENERAL MACALLISTER IS A FASCIST PIG—in huge blood-red letters in the pale-green corridor. She heard of it later, after some young child had innocently pointed the accusing finger and Dwight had admitted his guilt. Colonel Allison offered to deal with him in a way he would never forget, but instead Dwight had to appear before the disciplinary committee. He was sentenced to twelve months' menial labor clearing raw sewage from the septic tanks and spreading it to dry on the river fields.

As for the rest of Bill Harnden's students who might share similar views . . . General MacAllister came personally to the schoolroom to deliver a lecture. For an hour and a half he went droning on about dangerous left-wing ideals and extreme socialist principles, about the threat to democracy that had resulted in nuclear war, and why subversive political activity would not be tolerated now. There was no such thing as freedom without order, General MacAllister said, just degeneration into lawless anarchy and social chaos.

"That's why I'm in authority, and why we have rules in this bunker!" General MacAllister barked. "We've got no room for deviants! Those of you who don't like the way things are run will have their chance to voice their complaints when the new parliamentary system has been established. We intend to keep the spirit of democracy alive. We of the military are here to protect the democratic principle. Meanwhile, a state of international emergency still exists that requires that we continue as we are."

But the continuation was not the same.

Dwight was banished from the schoolrooms.

And gone from Ophelia's life.

"I hope you're satisfied!" Erica said to Bill. "I told you this would happen! That boy was at an impressionable age and you encouraged him in his foolish thinking!"

"I taught him to think for himself, that's all."

"And what good has it done him?"

"Let's hope," said Bill, "it will make him a better man."

"Or waste what he could have been!"

Ophelia did not know what Dwight had become or what effect the punishment was having on him. She seldom saw him anymore. With the sounding of the eight-o'clock work buzzer, he donned his white protective suit and went outside, day after day amid the dung and dust, creating a few more fertile acres that might one day grow. Ophelia knew only what Wayne told her—that Dwight not only smelled shitty, he was also a shit to live with, and all he and Colonel Allison did was yell at one another.

It was Erica who told her that Dwight had been moved to a single room on the opposite side of the underground complex. And it was Erica, more than her father, who seemed to understand how Ophelia felt, bereft and purposeless, her life become empty of meaning. She had to find something for herself, said Erica. Become a complete person within herself and not rely on relationships to make her whole and happy. Love from a member of the opposite sex was not the be-all and end-all of a woman's existence.

"You don't need Dwight Allison to become a good geneticist," Erica said. "You can do that quite well without having him around."

Genetics was not everything, Ophelia thought. Without Dwight she could feel no pleasure. There were no more baseball games. The storage depot was abandoned, and socially the group drifted apart, split into individuals, pairs, or trios of particular friends. It was as if Dwight had been the one who kept them together, motivated their activities, molded them into a unity. Without him they lacked cohesion and had nothing in common. All the life and laughter of joint enterprises seemed to be gone. Weekends and evenings were long and boring, and Ophelia bit her fingernails until they bled.

"Will you stop doing that!" her father said.

"What else is there to do?" Ophelia asked bitterly.

"Try learning," he replied.

"You're already using the computer, so how can I?"

In the swivel chair Bill swung around to face her. The screen behind him showed an extract from *Macbeth*. Ophelia wanted to hate him, because she believed, like Erica, that what had happened to Dwight was all his fault. But a photograph fluttered to the floor and she picked it up. She had seen it before. It was a photograph of her father's previous family, a smiling woman with two young children and a girl of her own age. For the first time Ophelia recognized the likeness between herself and Sarah. She might have been staring at her own face.

"She even bit her nails and chewed her lip like you do," said Bill. "And I didn't mean academic learning. I was thinking of the lesson of experience."

Ophelia handed him the photograph.

"Did you love her?" she asked.

"Sarah?" he said.

"Veronica," said Ophelia.

"I loved them all," he said simply.

"But you don't love Mommy, do you?"

Bill sighed.

"Sometimes I think she doesn't want to be loved," he said. "Or maybe she does but doesn't know it. Or maybe there are things that are more important than love. Respect, for instance. I've a great deal of respect for your mother, however much I may disagree with her. And growing up is always a painful process, whatever age you're at."

Ophelia stared at him in astonishment.

"Mommy's fifty-seven!" she said.

"And I'm sixty-six," said Bill. "But I haven't stopped learning. Minds continue to evolve. When evolution stops, the species dies, and that applies to individuals

as well. Both as individuals and as a species, we have
been lucky to escape extinction, but we cannot afford
to stand still. Sorrow is wisdom, the poet said. However bad the experience, we can always learn something from it. And that applies to us all, Ophelia. Me
and Erica, as well as you and Dwight. It's just people
like MacAllister who never learn."

"Mommy believes he's right," Ophelia said quietly.
Bill shrugged.

"In that case you must make up your own mind."

ooo

The small convoy of army trucks left for Milford Haven
and returned five days later loaded with supplies of
gasoline. Now, for the first time in seven years, the
helicopter was able to make a full aerial survey. Photographs taken over Wiltshire and Gloucestershire and
Somerset showed the latest information on refoliation,
reforestation, bird life, animal life, and the small communities of human survivors. Progress reports were
updated, relevant details relayed to the Berkshire
Bunker for inclusion in central government records,
and Bernard Sowerby had to begin all over again with
the maps.

Like everyone else, Ophelia heard that the Somerset
levels were beginning to recover, the acres of peat
bogs and water meadows showing green again. Mi-
gratory birds nested among the osier beds and raised
their young. Several hundred people in three small
villages grew wheat and potatoes in fields on the edge
of the marshes. Sheep grazed in the Cotswold valleys,
and two small wool mills seemed to be working. There

were communities on the Quantocks and the Mendip Hills, and on the edges of Exmoor. Fishing boats operated out of Watchet and Minehead, and the goat population that grazed the Wiltshire Downs had increased in numbers. But the gray-black deserts were still the dominant feature, Bernard Sowerby said, and except on the river margins nothing grew in the county of Avon, and no people lived there but themselves.

The time had come, General MacAllister decided, to start looking outward. There was enough grass on the river fields to support a sizeable flock of sheep. A small herd of cattle had been spotted in the hills of West Gloucestershire beyond the river Severn.

"Bring them in," MacAllister ordered Colonel Allison. "I want those cattle here under government protection."

That same evening Dwight re-entered Ophelia's life. Just after they had returned from dinner in the dining hall, he came bursting into their apartment. He was taller than she remembered, leaner and stronger, with healed blisters on the palms of his hands. He was obviously angry about something and did not speak to her or Erica.

"Have you heard the latest?" he asked Bill.

"What in particular, Dwight?"

"MacAllister's requisitioning the outsiders' cattle. Every last one of them, Wayne said. Pop received orders this afternoon. They're loading them into the army trucks and transporting them back here."

Erica slipped on her white laboratory overalls.

Her eyes glittered behind her glasses.

"With fresh supplies of animal protein we can guarantee our survival," she said. "We'll be able to increase the population of the bunker."

"What about the survival needs of the outsiders?" Dwight asked angrily. "To hell with them, I suppose?"

"They're in our administrative district," Erica explained. "It's no different from people paying taxes before the war, or tithes to the church. They may not like it, but that's how the system works."

"Then the system is immoral!" Dwight said furiously. "It's blasted serfdom! Class division! History repeating itself! What gives us the right to set ourselves up over them? Let them to do all the donkey work and take what we want? Even Pop says it stinks!"

Erica tried to tell him. What belonged to the government belonged to all people. That way resources would be shared equally and not be enjoyed by just a few. That was not how it had been before the holocaust, Dwight argued. Equal sharing had never been a quality displayed by Western civilization. Their whole society had revolved around personal greed, the amassing of goods and money by individuals and nations. Even within the rich industrial countries the poor, and the sick, and the unemployed had not gotten much of a share. And in the rest of the world millions were left to starve!

Erica shrugged. The requisitioning of supplies by the government was common practice during a national crisis, she said. For the sake of the nation individuals were expected to make personal sacrifices. And it was a fact of life, even among animal communities, that some were born to lead and others to follow. Dwight should be thankful he had been born to a privileged position inside the bunker, she said.

"The biggest load of autocratic hogwash I've ever heard!" said Dwight. "It's just a bloody excuse! The concept of social superiority among people is a corruption of animal practices! And I'm not a baboon, even if you are!"

"Cool it," said Bill. "That was uncalled for."

Dwight rounded on him.

"You were the one who taught me to think before I swallowed bullshit! And if that's not bullshit, I don't know what is! You heard what she said! Tell her, for Christ's sake! We can't let MacAllister get away with this act of banditry!"

"Just cool it," Bill repeated.

"We've got to *do* something!" Dwight said.

Bill held up his hands in a gesture of surrender.

"Okay, I agree with you. Let's concentrate on that, shall we? Let's talk about what we can do, calmly and constructively. Firstly we need a general consensus on the issue. Then we need a joint decision on what action we are prepared to take—a withdrawal of labor maybe."

"I'm not listening to this!" Erica snapped.

"We need to discuss it," said Bill.

"I want no part in it!" Erica shouted. "You go ahead and discuss it, if that's what you want, but leave me out of it! I'm going to the laboratory. I've been insulted enough for one evening!"

She stormed out and slammed the door.

In the room there was silence.

"I'm sorry," said Dwight. "I shouldn't have called her a baboon."

"Take a seat," Bill said wearily.

Dwight flumped down on the vacant chair. Foam rubber stuffing oozed from a split in the red-plastic covering, and the air conditioning softly hummed. White words glowed on the small computer screen before Bill reached over and turned it off. Ophelia bit her fingernails and waited. She did not know whose side she was on, or if she agreed with Erica or Dwight.

"Pop's leaving at first light," said Dwight.

"Which doesn't give us much time," said Bill.

"Suppose we warned them?"

"MacAllister and company are not likely to listen."

"No," said Dwight. "Suppose we warned the outsiders."

"That would mean stealing an army truck," said Bill.

"And I can't drive," said Dwight.

"But I can," said Bill.

"Are you with me?"

"Do we know where these cattle are?"

"Bernard Sowerby can photocopy a map. I think it's a place called Dean, in West Gloucestershire."

"I know it," said Bill.

"Daddy used to live there," said Ophelia.

For the first time since he had entered the room, Dwight actually looked at her, noticed she was there.

"We're going to have to leave before morning," he said. "Can you swipe us some travel rations from the canteen kitchen?"

Ophelia made up her mind.

If Dwight and her father were leaving, then so was she, and it had nothing to do with right or wrong, or whom she believed. It was not a decision. It was instinct.

"I'll get the rations," Ophelia said. "And you can get

the protective suits. Daddy's size twenty, and I'm a size fourteen."

"You're not coming!" said Dwight.

"You're not leaving me here!"

"This isn't a blasted joyride!"

"I'm coming," Ophelia said stubbornly. "And you can't stop me . . . unless you want me to go and tell General MacAllister what you're about to do? I'm not staying here anyway, not without Daddy. Something might happen, and nobody knows what outsiders are like. So I'm coming with you. Tell him, Daddy!"

"I guess she's coming with us, Dwight," said Bill.

∘∘∘

Like many others, Colonel Allison believed that the leadership of every bunker should be democratically elected, that General MacAllister had hung on to his position for long enough. But unlike Dwight, he was no revolutionary. Orders were orders, he said, and if he did not carry them out then someone else would. Dwight and Bill must do what they thought to be right, and so must he.

"You won't report them, Jeff?" Mrs. Allison said anxiously.

"The whole thing is distasteful enough without that," said Colonel Allison. "If those cattle are gone by the time I get there, then I'm not answerable. Whatever you choose to do, Harnden, I know nothing about it."

"We need a truck," said Dwight.

"The keys are in the ammunition room," said Colonel Allison. "And the trucks are all tanked up. Better take a rifle while you're about it. Those wild dogs are not only savage, they're rabid. The key to the ammunition room is in the top drawer of my desk. Think I'll stroll on down to the recreation room for a game of pool."

The door closed behind him.

And Dwight took the keys.

"I've got to do it, Mom," he said.

Mrs. Allison smiled sadly.

Then looked at Ophelia and Bill.

"What about Erica?" she asked.

"I'm not sure I can tell her," said Bill.

"If you do," said Dwight, "we'll get no farther than the main tunnel. She *wants* those cattle brought here."

Mrs. Allison frowned.

"You two can go," she said to Dwight and Ophelia. "I have a few things to say to Bill, in private."

Dwight and Ophelia went to the armory. They stole the ignition keys for the lead truck parked in the tunnel, plus a submachine gun and ammunition belt. They stole food and water bottles from the canteen and returned to wait in the apartment. They were already dressed in their white protective suits when Bill arrived. He too dressed in a white protective suit as Dwight shouldered the backpack, and Ophelia carried the gun. It was twenty to midnight by the apartment clock.

"We should have a clear eight-hour start," said Dwight.

"You go ahead," said Bill.

"What do you mean?" Ophelia asked in alarm.

"I mean wait for me in the truck. I'll be along in a minute," said Bill.

"What's the holdup?" Dwight asked suspiciously.

Erica opened the door. She had returned early from the laboratory, and Ophelia's heart sank. They did not need to tell her their intention. It was obvious they were leaving, going outside. But Erica's reaction was not what Ophelia expected, no scathing remarks, no blazing anger, no recriminations or blame, just a broken desperate glance at her only daughter before she crossed the room, rested her head on Bill's shoulder, and started to cry.

Dwight hustled Ophelia from the room.

"That's no place for us," he said.

"But what's the matter with her?" Ophelia asked.

"Use your imagination!" Dwight said.

Chewing her lip, Ophelia followed him along the corridor. The lighting was dimmed at night to conserve energy, and there was no one about. Apartment doors were closed and most people slept. And it had never been necessary to guard the bunker at night, because the outer doors could be opened only from the inside. Dwight entered the console room and pulled the release lever, then led Ophelia on past the dining hall and storage depot, along the sidewalk of the main tunnel until they reached the leading army truck. She watched him stow the gun and kitbag in the back with two drums of gasoline, then climbed into the cab and sat beside him to wait. It was eerie and quiet. Moonlight shone at the end of the tunnel and his fingers drummed restlessly on the steering wheel.

"What's taking Daddy so long?" she asked.

"Sometimes," said Dwight, "you're so thick I can hardly believe it."

"If you're so damned clever, why don't you tell me?"

"What the hell do you think they're doing?" said Dwight. "How would you feel if the man you had lived with and loved for twenty years suddenly decided he was leaving? We won't be coming back, you know."

Ophelia looked at him in alarm.

"What do you mean? Of course we'll be coming back!"

Dwight turned on the ignition. His face showed green by the dashboard lights, and it had never occurred to Ophelia that Erica might care, or that they might be leaving forever. "What do you mean about not coming back?" she repeated. And Dwight had to spell it out for her. He said they were burning their boats as far as General MacAllister was concerned, defecting to the other side, political traitors and enemies of the state. He said that unless MacAllister was ousted they would have to seek political asylum among the outsiders. Traitors, said Dwight, were either imprisoned, executed, or excommunicated from the society in which they lived.

Ophelia had not thought of that. She had not thought of anything much. It was emotion that had driven her, a need to be with her father because he was the only person who had ever really loved her. Or maybe she had wanted to be with Dwight, and that was emotional too. Doubts besieged her. She did not really want to leave the bunker, and she certainly did not want to spend the rest of her life among outsiders. Maybe she ought to stay with Erica? Maybe other things were more important than her need to be loved? Maybe it was not too late to change her mind? But her father climbed into the cab and the engine roared into life. Sick fear gripped her as the truck emerged into the vast abandoned darknesses of earth and sky, headed toward an unimaginable future below unknown stars.

"Is Erica okay?" Dwight asked.

"She won't tell, if that's what you mean," said Bill.

"No," said Dwight. "That's not what I meant. I mean is she all right?"

Bill raised his voice above the roar of the engine.

"The conflict between personal loyalty and public duty is something she's never had to cope with before. I left her with your mother."

"Good old Mom," Dwight said bleakly. "She'll stand by anyone, even me."

"We *are* doing the right thing," Bill assured him.

"Are we?" said Dwight. "Right for us and right for the outsiders, maybe. But not right by MacAllister according to central government policy."

" 'To thine own self be true,' " said Bill.

"In spite of the majority?"

"Once upon a time," said Bill, "the majority believed the world was flat. They crucified Christ and allowed the nuclear war to happen. Individuals give rise to new majorities, Dwight."

Dwight laughed.

"These last six months spent spreading shit I actually thought it was me who was crazy. I reckoned that if guys like MacAllister were sane, then I had got to be mad. Nice to know I'm not the only nut case."

"It seems there are three of us," Bill replied.

Am I? thought Ophelia.

And physically she was with them.

But in her mind she was totally alone.

ooo

It was five o'clock on a summer's morning and they
had been traveling all night, northward along the line
of the highway with endless detours around the rubble
of its bridges. Bright stars had shone on an alien land-
cape where the wind whipped up clouds of dust, and
the noise of the engine, the smell of gasoline, and the
shuddering vibrations of the truck were making Ophelia feel sick. Now the low sun dazzled her eyes, and
she lowered the tinted visor of her helmet, and the
road dissolved among the blackened vitrified remains
of factories and housing complexes and flattened miles
of wreckage.

"Gloucester," said her father.

Dwight studied the map.

"We'll have to go around it," he said.

"Can't we stop for a while?" Ophelia begged.

"We'll stop when we reach the river," said Bill.

The truck drove on toward barren hills, lurched
and jolted over tussocks of grass, fallen masonry, and
crumbling concrete. Horizons swayed and tilted, and
dust grimed the windshields. They were searching for
the tracks of the convoy trucks that had traveled this
way to Milford Haven, but weeks of weather had erased
all traces. Sunlight shimmered over the ruins of the
city and over the black deserts surrounding it, and the
sky was so blue it hurt to see. Time passed and heat
built up inside the cab.

"I've got to get out!" Ophelia said desperately.

"Not yet," said Dwight.

"I'm going to be sick!"

He leaned across her and wound down the window. "Do it out there," he said.

Neither he nor her father seemed to care how sick she was, they only cared about reaching the outsiders before Colonel Allison. Ophelia heaved up bile along a stretch of moving asphalt. Dust blew in her eyes and the landscape turned watery, a black molten desert where fence posts trailing wire marked the boundaries of what had once been fields. A rusting yellow road sign, twisted and broken, said that the road they were on was the Golden Valley Bypass.

"We're too far north!" shouted Dwight.

Bill reversed the truck in a scream of tires on dust. In mid heave Ophelia fell backward and was sick on the floor of the cab. Dwight was furious. "I couldn't help it!" Ophelia wept. And still her father drove on, heading back toward Gloucester.

It seemed like hours before they reached the river. Noise in the silence screamed in Ophelia's head. The stink stayed in her nostrils and her legs felt like jelly as Bill led her down the bank. Dwight was already filling a container with muddy water to clean out the cab, and if looks could have killed, Ophelia would have been dead. But she was past caring. She lay among damp earth and rushes, stripped of her white protective suit. The arched shadows of Telford's bridge kept off the blistering effects of the sun's rays, and the river swirled by her, leaving its traces on her ungloved hands.

She sluiced her face, sat with her head on her knees, and waited. Long slow minutes trickled away, but finally the echoes of the engine noise faded away and other sounds took over. She could hear her father talking and Dwight pumping air into the front tires, yet they were lost among the silences and the soft running music of the river. The queasy churning of her stomach was gone into the stillness where lace-winged flies danced in the sunlight and fish bubbles broke the surface. Brown water whirled and eddied with trails of green weed. A dragonfly flashed turquoise and insects sang, and a small flower crushed by her fingers gave off a sweet elusive scent. The flowers were everywhere under her, a spreading purple mat of sheer fragrance.

Ophelia gazed in a kind of wonderment. Sense impressions she had never dreamed of, never imagined, stirred and awoke and were overwhelmed. This was the world that had been destroyed, the world her father talked of—scents and sights, colors and sounds, the sweet fresh air and the green glory of grass. It was a little strip of paradise beside an English river where life was beginning again. A little brown bird warbled on a branch of springing willow, and the dragonflies danced.

" 'A thing of beauty is a joy forever.' "

Those were the words her father had taught her, and she had never understood what they meant until now. Back at the bunker there was no beauty like this. Here there was a wallflower growing from the old stones of the bridge, living petals, yellow streaked with scarlet, and the flies above the water like winged jewels. Ophelia would have liked to stay there forever, but the shadow of Dwight fell darkly on the grass beside her.

"Feeling better?" he asked.

"What do you care?" Ophelia said angrily.

"We've got to move on," said Dwight.

"We've only just got here! And why don't we move from the bunker and settle somewhere like this?"

"The river floods in spring and autumn," Dwight informed her.

"Somewhere else then?"

"It's not easy living outside," Dwight said.

He squatted beside her, stared at his hands, callused and hard with the healed scars of blisters. Even above the smell of gasoline Ophelia was aware of the sewery stink that seemed to be ingrained in him. Dwight had been working outside long enough to know the back-breaking labor entailed in trying to make the desert grow. She understood what drove him to protect the outsiders.

But she still clung to a different dream . . . the dream of an underground city with flowers, and water gardens, and trees growing under artificial sunlight, and birds and animals and people. She dreamed of the bunker as an oasis of life slowly spreading outward until the whole of England was green again. She realized that Avon was not an ideal situation, that the bunker needed to be elsewhere, but unlike Dwight she was not prepared to give up on it and face the struggle outside.

They crossed the Severn by Telford's bridge, which was the only one left standing, and Dwight took the wheel. Learning to drive the truck meant traveling slowly along roads of dust between dead hedges and abandoned villages as they headed west toward the borders of Wales. A hot summer wind blew through the open windows, and on the river's flood plain the grass had dried brown, supporting nothing but a few skinny sheep that roamed across the miles. They saw dogs in the distance but no signs of people, nor any sign of pursuit. But somewhere behind they knew the convoy trucks would be following, qualified army drivers who could make up time and already knew the route.

○○○

Ophelia slept for a while with her head on her father's shoulder, and when she awoke they were driving among rugged hills where gaunt skeletons of dead trees were still standing. Bare branches trailed dark ivy, sucking a little life from the ruined earth. Here and there amid the burnt black ashes were fronds of green bracken, patches of grass, and a few pink foxglove flowers. Rabbits with blind white eyes bolted away, and the village houses were almost intact, black gaps of doors and windows and sagging roofs. Rooms and gardens were choked with stinging nettles and bramble mounds, leaves of elder hanging limp in the heat and gray with dust. All these alien plants Bill recognized and named, but Ophelia was feeling ill again. Waves of sickness washed over her, and she sweated inside her white protective suit.

"I want to get out," she said faintly.

"Just a few more miles," said Bill.

Roads had reverted to wilderness, and the truck swerved and jolted over rough ground as Dwight detoured to avoid a fallen tree, shuddered up the slope, and rumbled down into the next valley.

Ophelia saw the village ahead, stone-built cottages where smoke billowed from the chimney stacks. Five skinny head of cattle grazed in a paddock by the stream.

Small fields grew wheat and potatoes and arable crops. Children, goats, and chickens wandered around the dusty compound of the street, scattered and fled as the truck drove in. People watched from the inside darkness of decaying rooms, and one little girl, blind and legless, heaved herself along on a makeshift wooden cart. Fat flies fed upon the festers of her eyes, and Ophelia fought down the sickness as Dwight stuck his head through the window and asked her the way.

The child pointed and the truck drove on past a stone quarry and a churchyard and an abandoned coal mine, and on again over the hills and down through the cracked streets of a deserted town. Surrounding hills were tinged with a pinkness of willow herb, and a few sapling birch trees grew among the forests of the dead. It was after noon by the sun and the heat was stifling, and the land her father had expected to recognize seemed unfamiliar and changed. He had to study the map.

"How much farther?" Ophelia moaned.

"Just a few more miles."

"You said that hours ago! And I bet that village was the place we were looking for."

"Five cows don't make a herd," said Bill.

"Which way now?" asked Dwight.

Then, from the top of the next rise, Ophelia saw the settlement before her. It was in a valley surrounded by hills, a collection of shacks, a few battered glass houses, and a stone-built cottage and barn. But the squalor was lost in the fields around it, acres of wheat and potatoes, rows of string beans and ripe red strawberries, and velvet-green pasture by the stream where the cattle grazed. Tall hedges of flowering elder made a mottled shade. There were willows by the water, and young trees foresting the hills beyond. Someone had cleared and planted. Someone had made the desert bloom in a glory of green. Ophelia could actually feel the coolness and peace of it.

"Johnson's place!" said Bill.

"You know it?" Dwight asked him.

"I've just this minute recognized where I am. It used to be a truck garden. I remember bringing Sarah here."

"It looks pretty well organized," said Dwight.

"So what are we waiting for?" Ophelia asked.

"They could be armed," said Dwight.

"Johnson was a pacifist," said Bill.

"It may not be Johnson, not after twenty years."

"So why don't we go and see?" Ophelia repeated.

The truck rattled and banged down the hillside, then lurched to a stop. Tangled fortifications of rusting barbed wire encircled the settlement. Half buried in gorse and bracken and brambles, it had been invisible to them from above. It was a trap for dogs and people alike, and barbed wire gates were padlocked against them, blocking the track.

"Doesn't look exactly friendly," said Dwight.

Bill put his hand on the horn, sound blasting through the heat and stillness and echoing around the surrounding hills. After a while they saw a woman coming toward them, walking slowly between bean fields scarlet with flowers. Her stomach was huge in the last weeks of pregnancy, and she was carrying a gun. Her sparse brown hair was uncombed, her dress thin and colorless after years of washing. Ophelia pushed up her visor, waited as Dwight and her father left the truck and went to meet her, watched as the woman leveled the gun. Her finger touched the trigger and it was aimed at Bill.

It was not fear of her father's death that made Ophelia cry out, tear off her protective helmet, and hurl herself from the cab. It was the sight of a face in the sunlight, burned red and blistering, hideously scarred, human deformity that made her instantly sick. At the foot of a gorse bush Ophelia heaved and vomited until she had nothing left to bring up. Liquid colors—leaf green, sky blue, and gold—slowly revolved and grew still. The journey was over and voices screamed through the still heat.

"Go away! There's nothing here for the likes of you!"

"You don't understand. We're here to warn you."

"We've given all we can and there's no more!"

"If we could speak to whoever's in charge?"

"My husband's ill! I'm telling you to go!"

"They're coming to steal your cattle!"

"No one steals! We give!"

Ophelia staggered toward the gate.

It did not matter how ugly the woman was.

She knew what it meant to suffer.

"Please," said Ophelia. "All I want is a drink of cold water and a place to lie down."

The woman looked at her. Blue human eyes gazed at her from the ulcerated remains of a face. Even in decay her eyes were still young, still capable of expression. Ophelia was not sure what she saw—disbelief, astonishment, recognition, even delight—but suddenly the woman dropped the gun, opened the gate, and held out her arms to embrace her.

"Sarah!" she cried. "You've come back! I thought you were dead! All these years I've been thinking you

were dead! Where have you been? And what happened
to William?"

Ophelia stared at her, backed away.

"It's me," she said. "Catherine! Your sister!"

"My God!" said Bill.

ooo

Dwight drove the truck down the track toward the
settlement, and Ophelia followed behind with Catherine and her father. Summer wind disturbed the scent
of elder flowers, set the green leaves dancing in flickers
of gold shade across her upturned face. The air was
liquid with lark songs over the hills and loud with the
hum of bees. There were hives by the river, Catherine
said, and all of this Johnson had made. He had dreamed
of a garden and made it grow from the dust.

They leaned on the gate leading into a walled field
full of potatoes, and her voice drifted through the wine-
sweet air of afternoon, Ophelia's new-found sister telling her story. It had not been easy, she said. They
had been thirty people crammed into one small cottage
through a nuclear winter twenty-four months long.
She remembered it well, the cold and the darkness
and the snow that buried the world.

She remembered the days before it had set in, going
with Johnson in a Land Rover fetching hay and cattle
feed for the calves. She had been alone with him then,
but as they had traveled around the farms and villages,
others had joined them. They hacked down trees to
keep the heating system running, and insulated the
shed to keep the generator from freezing. But the
lights had stayed burning in the glass houses where

the plants grew and the animals were kept. They dug tunnels in the snow, and lived on goats' milk, eggs, beans, and potatoes.

People had survived in other places too. Some had taken livestock into their homes, people and animals sharing the same warmth. Some had eaten dead meat frozen in the snow, rats and corpses, insects and worms, rotting vegetables and even manure. Even when the winter was over it was not easy. There was disease, and sickness, and starvation, and babies were born deformed. But slowly, over the years, they had consolidated their hold on the land and established separate communities.

Things were getting better, Catherine said. They produced enough food to see them through the winter, ground their own flour, and baked bread in the fire ovens. They did not kill animals for meat except when they were old or sickly, but nobody went hungry or cold. They had learned to spin sheep's wool, dye, knit, and weave. They made waterproof clothes out of goatskins, shoes out of cowhide, willow baskets, clay pots, and herbal remedies.

"We're hoping to build a communal living house," said Catherine. "Johnson said it will be easier to run than individual homes. The old nuclear family system didn't work, so we're going to live and work together. Before the war each family was isolated, which destroyed the spirit of the community. At least, that's how Johnson sees it."

"Johnson sounds like a remarkable man," said Bill.

"He is," said Catherine. "Quite remarkable. He thought of everything. When the snows receded, he took the Land Rover for a trip to the local libraries and brought back all the books we were likely to need. People come here if they want to know anything, and Johnson teaches them, from the books. We're a kind of distribution center. I think we've supplied almost every settlement in the area with seeds and livestock, although not all of them have cattle yet. Johnson believes that the stuff of life, like knowledge itself, belongs to all people, and we have no right to keep things to ourselves. Right from the beginning, however little we had, we always shared it."

"The true spirit of communism," her father murmured.

"Yes," said Catherine. "But now Johnson is dying."

"I'm sorry to hear that."

"We shall miss him," Catherine said simply.

She spoke of Johnson as of a holy man, with reverence in her voice. Yet Ophelia knew that nobody was perfect. She had only to look at Catherine, her weeping sunburn and rotting teeth, stringy hair that failed to conceal the radiation sores that festered on her scalp, to see that ugliness and suffering still existed, even here in the garden paradise Johnson had created.

"Is this your first child?" Bill asked.

Catherine laughed.

"I've had seven," she said. "But they all died except for Lilith. But I pray each day that this baby will survive, for Johnson won't live long enough to father another."

Bill looked at her in horror.

"You're *married* to Johnson?"

"Since I was fourteen," said Catherine.

"And how old was he?"

Catherine shrugged.

"Forty, maybe? Does it matter? I was mature and lived with him and we cared for each other. It was natural to mate. What else could we have done?"

Ophelia stared at her. The loveliness of the valley, the sanctity of its life, fled to a hideous reality. It was horrible, unthinkable . . . sexual intercourse between a fourteen-year-old girl and a forty-year-old man . . . breeding like animals, having no choice, pregnancy after pregnancy, and all the children dying. Catherine's great swollen stomach seemed suddenly obscene, the result of one more sordid act of conception. Ophelia's lips set in a prim line of disgust as she walked away down the track. At least in the bunker they had kept morality alive. And the green growing fields ended abruptly in a compound of dust.

Nothing beautiful remained, just battered glass houses, a run-down cottage and ramshackle barns, and the settlement beyond. It was a scene of absolute squalor. Hundreds of wooden shacks with plastic windows and rusting corrugated roofs faced across the sun-baked spaces where the army truck was parked. Garden sheds, she heard her father saying. And people actually lived in them! Over seven hundred people, Catherine said, although most of them were away in the hills picking bilberries, or quarrying for stone for the new communal living hall. The stink was terrible. Flies buzzed around the primitive latrines and rats frisked across the garbage dump, white eyes winking in the light.

It was no wonder Catherine's babies died!

No one could live in conditions like these!

The land came first, Catherine said, food and necessities before material advancement and academic learning. They would not be living like this forever, she said, and pointed out the foundation trenches for the new building. Meanwhile among the germs and dirt a woman sang and small children cried. Fowls bathed in the dust and goats chewed their cuds in the wooden shade of the sheds before the valley grew green again, curved with the stream between hills where the bright woods brooded, and the willow herbs bloomed sweet.

A mixture of feelings tore Ophelia apart. She saw the coexistence of hope and despair, beauty and ugliness, the profane and the sublime. Caught between wonder and loathing, she walked through the reek of dung and flowers to stand beside Dwight in the shadow of the army truck.

"What do you think of it?" he asked her.

"I think it stinks!" Ophelia said savagely.

"Figuratively? Or literally?"

"Both! It makes me feel absolutely sick! At least we've managed to maintain a decent standard of living! At least we're still capable of civilized behavior!"

"Like coming to steal their cattle?" said Dwight. "You call that civilized? We're dinosaurs in a bunker! We deserve to become extinct!"

Ophelia stared at him.

"What do you mean?" she said.

"What I said!" he retorted. "And what did you expect? The celestial city?"

ooo

In the kitchen Dwight pumped water into a cracked china sink and sluiced his face as Ophelia followed her father into the living room. Just for a moment, after the blinding sunlight outside, she could see nothing. But slowly the room took shape—chairs and a table, an old-fashioned fire grate, ragged curtains at the window, and remnants of a carpet on the floor, books stacked in every available space. The air was heavy with the smell of books. And in the midst of them, reclining on a battered sofa, was a bearded man, a skin-and-bones shape clad in nothing but a pair of faded denim shorts.

"This is Johnson," Catherine said fondly.

He looked so old, many years older than Ophelia's father. His scalp, like Catherine's, was covered with festering sores. He tried to rise, but his strength failed. Breath rattled in his throat as he sank back against the cushions. One skeletal hand extended in greeting as Bill stepped forward.

"My father," said Catherine.

Johnson coughed and nodded.

His teeth were gone.

But his voice was strong and sure.

"We've met before, I think, but I forget your name. Two boxes of pansies, wasn't it?"

" 'Pansies, that's for thoughts,' " Bill quoted. "Just call me Bill. And this is Ophelia, my other daughter."

"I thought she was Sarah," Catherine explained.

Johnson smiled. "The fair Ophelia," he said. "How beautiful you are. I had forgotten how beautiful the human face could be."

Ophelia wanted to hate him. She wanted to hate him for all he had done to Catherine, for all the corruption she had found in the heart of this valley. But he was dying, and Catherine was a woman now. Twenty-eight, she had told her father. Her hand touched Johnson's, and his eyes softened with affection. He called her his darling Kate, and asked her to make some tea. He seemed to radiate a kind of inner light, a transparency of warmth and love it was impossible to hate.

"First," said Catherine, "I must take Ophelia upstairs and find her a bed."

"She's ill?" Johnson asked anxiously.

"It's only travel sickness," Ophelia said.

"Come," said Catherine, and held out her hand.

Ophelia followed her reluctantly, up a dim wooden stairway and into an upper room. Dusty sunlight filtered through the grimy window, and the crumpled sheets on a vast double bed were stained and torn. Peeling wallpaper showed a pattern of fading flowers. From a chest of drawers Catherine took out clean linen, stripped off the bed covers, winced in pain, straightened, and clutched her back.

"You'd better let me do that," Ophelia said.

She remade the bed as Catherine cleared the floor of soiled clothes and found her a nightgown. It was blue nylon with tattered lace edges.

"It's my best," said Catherine. "But you're welcome to borrow it. The bathroom is next door. There's septic-tank drainage and a flush toilet, the only one on the site. When Lilith returns, I'll ask her to make you a cure for your sickness. I'll just go and fetch you a glass of water."

"You shouldn't be waiting on anyone in your condition," Ophelia told her.

Catherine smiled.

"It's a perfectly normal condition for a woman, and I've Lilith to help me when she gets home. You lie down and rest."

"You're the one who should be resting," Ophelia objected.

Catherine sighed.

"It wouldn't make any difference," she said. "I've been through it enough times before. The little one's fate has nothing to do with rest and nourishment. It's genetics, Johnson says. We're genetically damaged, you see. Lilith laid the last one outside in the snow. Better a quick death than weeks of suffering. The poor little thing was too deformed to live for very long, and Lilith always sees what chance of life a baby has. Sometimes I think she sees too much, but Johnson says we have to heed her, however hard it seems."

It was horrible! Everything about this place was horrible! Lilith had killed her own mother's child, and Ophelia did not want to meet her. She wanted to go home, back to the bunker, blot out everything she had heard and seen. Her head ached violently. Her stomach churned, and voices murmured in the rooms below.

"Will you ask Daddy to bring my water?" Ophelia said. "I want to talk to him."

Catherine nodded, opened the windows, drew the curtains, and went downstairs. Ophelia undressed, put on the blue nylon nightgown, and lay on the bed. The clean sheets smelled of lavender. Sleepy afternoon sounds of birds and children drifted in from outside, and the curtains fluttered in the breeze. Cool shade surrounded her. She wanted to sleep, but she had to wait for her father. She had to tell him that no matter what happened, no matter what the punishment was, she wanted to go home, back to the bunker, away from this cruel outside world that she could not bear.

◦◦◦

When Ophelia awoke the room was dim with shadows. It must have been evening by the smells of smoke and cooking, the noise and bustle of the settlement outside. But the room contained its own silence, and she was suddenly aware that she was not alone. Ophelia turned her head. A skinny, flaxen-haired girl stood beside her bed with a cup in her hand. In the dusky half-light Ophelia could not see her clearly, just the pale oval of her face, the smudges of her eyes, a wraithlike figure in a shapeless gray dress. Ophelia sat up.

"I asked Daddy to bring my water," she said.

The girl stared at her, unseen eyes taking her in. She pointed to the bedside table, where a glass of water stood, then thrust the cup into Ophelia's hands and gestured her to drink.

"What is it?" Ophelia asked suspiciously.

The gesture was repeated, and Ophelia drank . . . liquid that was strong and bitter and as cold as ice. An herbal brew. Something to cure the sickness, Catherine had said. It tasted horrible, but she felt the still, imperious gaze of the girl fixed on her face, ruthlessly commanding her to finish every last drop. Then she took back the cup and turned to go. Light from the passageway touched her eyes, the blank whiteness of the congenitally blind. Radiation damage. She had obviously been born dumb as well as blind. Just for a moment Ophelia pitied her, until the girl paused in the doorway and looked back. Fear crawled through the nerves of her stomach. She got the feeling that the girl was not blind at all, that she could see everything Ophelia was, and the pity was all on her.

"Are you Lilith?" she asked.

And the girl nodded her head.

∘∘∘

Morning sun lay bright outside the window, but sleep sucked at Ophelia's mind and she had to struggle to open her eyes. Her father was shaking her, ordering her to wake, trying to tell her something. Cattle and childbirth and Colonel Allison were all mixed up together. She was drugged, and dozy, unable to understand. He had to shake her again and make her sit up.

"Are you listening?" asked Bill.

"Lilith," muttered Ophelia.

"She's downstairs. Catherine's in labor and Colonel Allison is on his way. I want you to keep an eye on Dwight. He's all steamed up and likely to do something stupid. Johnson and I are going to try reason, and Dwight's not in the mood for that. You'll have to keep him out of the way . . . take him for a walk, or something."

"But what about the cattle?" Ophelia asked.

"I've just told you!" said Bill. "What's the matter with you? They're dairy cows mostly, and in-calf heifers. We couldn't get them away because there's nowhere to drive them to, nowhere else with enough grass to feed a herd that size. We got the stud bulls away last night, but the rest are still here." Bill tossed her clothes on the bed. "Just take care of Dwight," he said. "That's all I ask."

"I want to go home," Ophelia stated.

"When this is over."

"Is that a promise?"

"Of course," Bill said impatiently. "I already promised your mother. There's work to do at the bunker, and you don't want to stay here, do you?"

He left and Ophelia sighed happily, lay back against the pillows, and closed her eyes. Erica had made Bill promise, and they would be going home. She did not care what happened now. Maybe she had never really cared, not even if Catherine *was* her sister. The problems of the outsiders were not her problems. They had problems of their own back at the bunker, and that was where Ophelia belonged, Dwight too. There was something she had to do about Dwight . . . something her father had told her, which she could not remember because all she wanted to do was sleep and sleep and sleep.

Downstairs someone was screaming. Ophelia shot out of bed, grabbed her underwear and overalls, and started to dress. Catherine was having the baby and she had to help, Bill had said. Her head was so muzzy she could hardly think. She went to the window and breathed in the chilly morning air. It was still early. The sky was changing from pearly pink to blue, the glass houses misted with condensation, the bean fields sparkling with dew. Johnson and her father were going slowly up the track and the settlement was coming awake, women collecting firewood from the stack, men emptying the lavatory buckets, and a solitary child drawing water from the well.

Ophelia stared at him, a stark, naked little boy of six or seven with bulbous joints and rickety legs. He seemed to be carrying something on his shoulders, a lolling fleshy growth the size of a human head. And then she saw that it *was* a head, a second head attached to a second neck, but only partly formed, a hideous fetal thing with a bulging brain. In pity and revulsion Ophelia turned away and went downstairs.

Lilith was sitting on the sofa where Johnson had lain. She sat with her hands in her lap as if she were waiting, an evil child who killed her mother's babies and put sleeping potions in people's drinks. Behind the closed sitting-room door Catherine moaned in pain and Ophelia knew whom Lilith was waiting for. She went through to the kitchen, where saucepans of water simmered on the wood-burning stove. Dwight was seated at the table eating bread and jam, and he did not even look at her.

"There's a boy outside," Ophelia began.

"I saw him," said Dwight.

"It made me feel sick."

"According to the midwife, they're all born deformed in one way or another," Dwight told her. "She's in there now seeing to your sister."

Ophelia helped herself to bread and jam.

"Lilith killed the last baby," she said. "She left it outside in the snow to die."

"Poor kid," said Dwight. "What strength she must have."

"She murdered it!" Ophelia said.

"Kinder," said Dwight. "Johnson told me last night. Not murder in their eyes, but mercy killing. Apparently they've practiced it since the beginning. Adults too, once they reach the last stages of dying."

He turned his head as Lilith entered the kitchen.

"Hi, Lilith. How's it going?"

And the horror smiled in answer to her name.

In the bright daylight Ophelia could see her quite clearly, her white-fair hair hanging straight and long, and pale downy hairs on her face and arms, almost like fur. She definitely was not blind. White eyes with black pinprick pupils fixed her with a cold repelling stare before she took the saucepan from the stove and carried it away. Once again Ophelia felt the fear. She had seen those eyes before in rats, and sheep, and rabbits. She recognized the significance.

"Lilith's a mutant," she said.

"That's evolution for you," said Dwight.

"You don't understand! The mutant gene is a dominant gene! Think what it means!"

"Her children will inherit her characteristics?"

"That's right. Eventually all outsiders will be mutants. Unless we can make a breakthrough in genetic engineering, we're going to be overrun."

"We've got no future anyway," said Dwight.

"What do you mean? Of course we've got a future! We've survived, haven't we?"

"Dinosaurs in a bunker," Dwight repeated. "We may have survived, but we haven't adapted. We're trying to cling to a life-style that is obsolete, and even our minds are stagnant. Our outlook hasn't changed since before the war. We couldn't exist outside that bunker, but these people can. They've learned to cope with changed conditions. It's the Liliths of this world who are going to survive in the long run, Ophelia. Not us."

From the inner room came a thin baby wail and an echo of girlish laughter, laughter that went on and on, a maniacal glee. Dwight was talking rubbish! Of course the human race was going to survive! Catherine had just given birth to a live healthy child and Ophelia was going to see.

The front sitting room was cramped and small. Books on shelves lined all the walls, and half-drawn curtains cut out the natural light. Candles in jam jars smelled of mutton fat, made glowing reflections in a gilt-framed mirror. On a bare scrubbed table the midwife was bathing the baby in a blue plastic bowl while Lilith watched and laughed, an insane gurgling sound. Her hands kept reaching to touch it as the midwife slapped them away. And in the corner of the room, on a mattress on the floor, Catherine lay amid the bloodstained aftermath of birth. What remained of her hair was matted with sweat, but her eyes were bright in the candlelight, shining with joy and relief.

"It's a girl, Ophelia," Catherine said. "Lilith's baby sister. She's fit and well and she's going to live. Isn't that wonderful?" She struggled to sit up. "Let me see her," she said to the midwife. "I want to show Ophelia my baby."

The midwife wrapped her in an old woollen shawl, brushed aside Lilith's clutching hands, and placed her in Catherine's arms. Gently she opened the shawl for Ophelia to see. The baby was naked, a pale little thing, completely covered in white silky hair, soft and thick as fur. Tiny fingers gripped when Ophelia touched her, and her eyes opened wide. They too were white. Black pinprick pupils seemed to drill through her mind, and the same fear shot through her. Just like Lilith the baby was a mutant albino thing.

"Isn't she beautiful?" said Catherine.

"Aye," said the midwife. "And more like her I have

birthed this year than any other, fine strong babies, all of them."

Genetic mutation, natural adaptation.

Suppose Dwight was right?

"She's very sweet," Ophelia said sickly.

And Lilith laughed.

○○○

Johnson was dying of radiation-induced cancer, and the walk up the track to meet Colonel Allison had left him exhausted. The cough racked his lungs, and he lay on the sofa with Lilith beside him, the baby cradled in his arms. Just for a moment his death did not matter, nor the fate of his cattle. He could still smile, still take delight from the sight of his new little daughter, Lilith's sister with her snow-white fur and milky eyes.

"Another little visionary," Johnson said softly.

"What will you call her?" asked Bill.

"Allison," said Johnson.

Colonel Allison shifted uncomfortably.

"You're naming her after me? After what I'm here to do?"

"I don't take it personally," Johnson said.

"You make me feel like a heel!" said Colonel Allison.

"Which is what you are," said Dwight.

"I didn't come here to argue with you, junior!"

"No," said Dwight. "You came here to thieve their cattle!"

Johnson gave the baby back to Lilith to return to her mother. Outside, the compound was full of men with rifles and white protective suits, and a dozen army trucks were parked on the hilltop. "Let's get down to business," Johnson said. And Colonel Allison placed the official requisition order on the table. The Avon Bunker, he explained, was the administrative head-quarters for the South West region, and the cattle would be transferred there to be reallocated through-out the whole administrative district.

"Like hell they will!" said Dwight. "They'll be real-located via MacAllister's gut, more like!"

"Is that my fault?" asked Colonel Allison.

"You're here, aren't you?"

"Me or someone else, what does it matter? You had your chance, junior. I gave you a clear twelve hours' start. Those cows should have been out of here and miles away by now."

"They're milkers," said Johnson.

"Nowhere else can handle such a herd," said Bill.

"I'm sorry about that," said Colonel Allison. "I really am. I don't much like what I have to do, but we'll load them onto the trucks after evening milking and be on our way. There will be compensation, of course, paid in pounds sterling. You can name your price."

"What good's that?" Dwight yelled. "What good are five-pound notes to these people except for wiping their backsides on?"

"When we get the economy going—" said Colonel Allison.

"Bullshit!" said Dwight. "You've got to be an idiot, Pop, if you believe that!"

"Let's not get carried away," said Bill.

"He's talking crap!" shouted Dwight.

"I'm under orders!" said Colonel Allison. "I've got no choice!"

"Everyone's got a choice, for Christ's sake! Even you! You've got a mind, Pop! Use it! Don't you care how many of these people are left to starve because of your actions? Screw MacAllister's beefsteak! Think about what you're doing! You're not bound to be a mindless cretin just because you've got some blasted stripes on your sleeve!"

"Keep on," said Colonel Allison, "and I'll give you a clip around the earhole, junior!"

"Why don't you go for a walk?" suggested Bill.

"I'll stop him if it's the last thing I ever do!" Dwight said viciously. "He'll not take those cattle if I have to kick his teeth in!"

"You're just not helping!" said Bill.

"Here," said Johnson, "we don't believe in violence, son. I appreciate what you're trying to do, but we'll handle it my way, thank you very much."

Dwight stared at him, sharp blue eyes in the sudden silence, then turned on his heel and left the room. Bill closed the door behind him. With Dwight out of the way they could get back to business, and Ophelia sighed. Part of her wished that Colonel Allison would load the cattle and leave immediately—then she too could go home. But there were seven hundred people at the settlement, dependent on those cattle, milk and butter and cheese, and Johnson was not about to relinquish what he had struggled twenty years to keep. Reallocation, Johnson explained, was already taking place. Eventually every settlement in the area would be supplied with cattle, and he was quite willing to widen his supply area to include Avon and the Cotswolds and anywhere else.

"That's reasonable," said Bill.

"Except that I'm not empowered to negotiate," said Colonel Allison.

"We can't handle a milking herd," said Bill. "We don't have the facilities."

"Central government policy clearly states—"

"Government?" said Johnson. "What government is this? I wasn't aware we had a government, and I certainly didn't vote for them. None of us did. You can't just walk in here, Allison, and expect me to believe you represent some government I've never heard of."

"I do have credentials."

"Credentials don't count," said Johnson. "I don't accept them, nor any other declaration of authority. No, Allison. The only power you have over us is force of arms. If you want those cattle, then you'll have to shoot the lot of us in order to take them, or else accept what I'm willing to give you—two milkers, six in-calf heifers, and one bull . . . the basis for a herd, and no more."

Ophelia yawned. Talk like this was liable to go on all day and already the sun was climbing toward noon. The settlement sweltered in the heat, and its stink wafted in through the open window. Outside the cottage the army truck Dwight had driven was ready to leave, and the soldiers waited for their final orders. Skylarks sang over the pink willow-herb hills and Colonel Allison was about to give in. He wanted more than Johnson offered but he was not an inhumane man. He was hardly likely to deprive seven hundred people of their livelihood. Or was he?

Ophelia was never to know. Shots rang out, the vicious rattle of a distant machinegun blasting through the outside silence, shattering speech and birdsong and Ophelia out of thought. A series of huge explosions shook the air as she and her father and Colonel Allison rushed outside. Men in white protective suits, who had been sheltering from the sun in the shade of walls, and half the population of the settlement, came running, everyone staring up the hillside to where the army trucks were parked. Black smoke billowed and flames licked the sky. The whole convoy was burning, and one solitary figure moved from the inferno and went running across the high horizon shouldering a gun.

"Dwight!" said Colonel Allison.

"No!" said Ophelia.

But she knew he was right.

Dwight had set the army trucks on fire.

White-suited men went pounding up the track.

Colonel Allison fired a revolver in the air.

"I want no killing!" he shouted. "Go after him and bring him back, but no killing! And see what's happened to Denton and Hargreaves! I left them guarding those trucks!"

The men waved, and saluted, and ran on.

"What now?" asked Bill.

"You can't drive milk cows across seventy-odd miles of desert," Colonel Allison said grimly. "MacAllister will have his guts for this, of course."

"Providing you catch him," said Bill.

Ophelia knew. Colonel Allison would never catch up with Dwight. He would lose himself in the wilderness of land and never come back. It was what he had intended, right from the beginning. Dinosaurs in a bunker, he had said. He thought the only future was here, but not for Ophelia. Her future was still in Avon, and the one remaining truck would take her back. She would go home, become a geneticist, and never see Dwight again.

Tears rolled down her cheeks and the sunlight burned her. She turned to go back inside. Lilith was standing in the doorway. Her eyes were narrowed in the light and she held the baby in her arms. Black pinprick pupils saw the fire, saw the grief on Ophelia's face, and slowly and pityingly she smiled.

PART THREE

SIMON

At dawn Simon took a rifle and a pair of binoculars and climbed the hill. The land looked dreary in the gray half-light, and a chill wind blew from the river estuary, stirred the miles of cotton grass, and whipped through the tatters of his white protective suit. Even after fifty-five years the toughened nylon still served its purpose, but the seams had rotted long ago and crude woollen stitches held it together. Scratches on the plastic visor impeded his vision and he raised it cautiously, watched the sky grow pink above the humped escarpment of the Cotswold Hills.

As the light brightened, the distances grew clear. He could see through the binoculars the wreckage of Avonmouth and the broken remains of the suspension bridge that had once spanned the river Severn. Water birds headed for the marshes, and a colony of seals were dozing on the mud flats. Directly below were the ruins of the town and the orange overnight tents where Harris and Sowerby were sleeping. A stone jetty at the river's edge dated back to Roman times, and the cross in the market square was even older. Celtic, Sowerby had said, and recently restored. Its dark shadow pointed toward him, or maybe to something behind.

Simon turned to look. Valleys dipped and hills rose before him, a rugged upland of gorse and heather, stunted bilberries, and withered skeletons of trees. Later they would be heading into it, and he raised his binoculars, hoping to see. There was a garden in a valley, his mother had said, green and fertile, where trees grew and cattle grazed. But all Simon saw were the ruins of yet another village and a single standing stone against the skyline.

It was time turning backward. Stones like that, which had marked the beginnings of civilization, now marked the end of it. No one in the bunker knew why the outsiders had resurrected the cromlechs, and monoliths, and stone circles, or how they had raised the giant blocks. Yet all over England the great stones marched across the trackless land, repeating the patterns of prehistory with uncanny precision. This one aligned with the Celtic cross behind him, and he guessed it went on across the river to Stonehenge. Everything led to Stonehenge, Sowerby reckoned.

" 'As it was in the beginning, is now, and ever shall be,' " Simon murmured.

Those stones had a power that had survived nuclear war and some things could never be destroyed. He shivered in the clear morning light, watched as a pack of dogs came over the hill. They hunted like wolves, scented and circled their prey, a goat, or a sheep, or maybe a person. A movement among the ruins of the village caught his eye and once more Simon focused the binoculars. The figure came clear, robed and hooded, kneeling in the dust among the crumbling walls of a building. He, or she, appeared to be digging, sifting through the debris of a dirt floor, searching for something, oblivious of danger. And the dogs closed in for the kill.

Simon did not stop to think. He aimed the rifle. Bullets ricocheted from the brickwork, pinged against the stones around the doorway, an immense rattle of sound that blasted through the silences. One dog lurched and fell. The others, shots whining around their ears, fled yelping and howling back up the hill to disappear over the horizon. And the silence returned with the calls of birds and the sigh of the wind through dry grasses.

Simon ran, his goatskin moccasins going soundless over the half mile of moorland. He stumbled over the stumps of ancient hedges, the wreck of a tractor, and the massed brambles of a buried farmyard. He was afraid of what he would find, that he had hit not only the dog but the person as well, killed what he had meant to save. Through old fields gone to wilderness he ran, along a track that must once have been a road, clambered over mounds of crumbling concrete and rotting timbers to reach the gap of the door.

The dog lay dead on the threshold, its white eyes glazed and blood staining the dust. Foam at its mouth suggested it was rabid, so he felt no guilt, just stepped across it and entered the room. Morning sunlight came through the window spaces, showed cupboards fallen from the walls, ferns growing in the sink unit, and nettles through the floor. Simon crossed to the inner doorway. The person was crouched in the sooty shadows of a fireplace, the pale smudge of a face and white robes covered with dirt.

"Are you all right?" he asked.

The girl held out her hand as if to ward him away.

"You will not shoot me!" she said.

Simon was not sure if it was a plea or a command, but he laid down his rifle, picked his way among the litter of digging tools and earth scrapes and fallen roof rafters. He thought she was hurt and went to touch her, but she shrank away from him, clutching the wall. Her voice sounded angry.

"You shouldn't be carrying a gun!"

"I wasn't shooting at you," Simon assured her.

"Weapons are evil!" she spat. "They are tools of the holocaust! There was a sound of thunder, and fire. Dust fell on the earth, and the darkness followed, and a great cold. All manner of creatures were destroyed. But the evil was gone. And the perpetrators of evil were gone. Gone forever, Lilith said. But you've brought it back! One of the evil ones!"

"I didn't mean to scare you," Simon said. "I was shooting at the dogs."

"You have no right to destroy a living thing!"

"If I hadn't shot it, you'd have been dead!"

"Would I?" asked the girl. "I doubt that."

She glanced toward the doorway, as if to make sure the dog was really there. But like most other creatures that had survived outside, her eyes were congenitally damaged, milky and opaque and probably blind, or so

Simon thought in a moment of pity. He held out his
hand.

"Let me help you up," he said.

"I can manage," the girl retorted.

She scrambled to her feet and brushed the soil from
her gown. It was fine white wool, handcrafted, with
exquisite designs in green and ocher around the edges.
Someone had made it. Someone had dyed and blended
those soft natural colors. In comparison the clumsy
stitches and uneven yarn of his own clothes might have
been fashioned by a five-year-old child. The girl might
hold some pretty primitive beliefs, but wherever she
came from, her people were skilled in other ways. He
noticed the goatskin bag dumped on the hearth stones,
fringed with fur and decorated with beads. He noticed
the fine beaten metal of her digging tools, a trowel
with a carved-bone handle, and fancy buckles on her
leather sandals. His own moccasins were crude and
shapeless, worn to holes after seventy miles of walking. No one in the bunker possessed clothes and ar-
tifacts like hers. Simon began to wonder what the word
"primitive" really meant.

Voices were calling him, borne by the wind across
the empty hillside. The older men, woken by the shooting, were coming to find him. But he stayed where he
was, staring at the girl, noting the significance. Grandfather Harnden had always said that in the bunker
they were teaching all the wrong things. He had been
an old man, soft in the head, and no one took much
notice of him, but suddenly Simon knew what he meant.
Compared to this girl he was the progeny of an almighty failure, people incapable of doing anything much,
and she with her blind white eyes fixed on his face

realized it too. She was not blind at all! Black pinprick pupils looked at him and saw, and he could feel her pity.

"Simon!"

The voices called and he backed away from her. He was used to people dying—his brothers and sisters of endemic diseases, some before he was even born, and his father dying of skin cancer. But he was not used to mutation. The girl was making him feel guilty, responsible for a war that had happened decades ago. It was people like him who caused the extinction of species and the birth of mutants like her. They had destroyed everything and preserved themselves . . . dinosaurs in a bunker, his mother said, with their rusting guns, drawing-board experts, and broken-down computers. It had been a kind of arrogance. But they were paying for it now, suffering for everything they had done and not done. Their numbers declined as the outsiders thrived, and that girl knew and pitied him.

"Don't look at me like that!"

"Simon! Where the hell are you?" Harris shouted.

He turned on his heel, picked up the gun and binoculars, and went outside. His visor was raised and the sunlight burned his face. Shards of broken masonry hurt his feet through the worn soles of his moccasins, and a rusty nail on a nearby gate post gashed his leg through his suit. Simon watched as the scarlet blood seeped through the white material and rapidly spread. People like him could rebuild cities, perform heart transplants, and travel to the moon . . . in theory. But when they had run out of tetanus injections, they had not been able to manufacture more.

ooo

It was only a gash, but Simon knew the implications
and he did not need Harris to spell it out. He could
lose not only his leg, but his life as well—gangrene,
lockjaw, septicemia. Not that Harris knew much about
it. He was a trained engineer, not a doctor. But he
was in charge of the expedition, and the survival of
many people depended on its outcome. If Simon got
sick, Harris would abandon him, and the blood still
ran in scarlet trickles down his leg.

"Can you walk?" Harris asked him.

"I'll need a compress," Simon replied.

"I'll go back to the camp," said Harris.

Sowerby and the girl came from the ruins.

"She says there's a healer nearby," Sowerby informed them.

"How far?" Harris asked anxiously.

The girl pointed to the standing stone.

"Three miles along the line, eleven point two five
degrees north of northwest."

"You mean they're compass lines?" asked Sowerby.

"Leave that until later," Harris told him. "We have
to go and gather up the gear. You wait here," he said
to Simon.

Harris and Sowerby walked away across the moorland, up the hill and down toward the camp, leaving
Simon alone with the girl. She squatted beside him,
dabbed at the blood with the hem of her dress, and
examined the wound. He noticed there were hairs on
the backs of her hands, fair and fine and thick as fur,

albino in the light. Simon recoiled with a feeling of horror. She was not human. She was a genetic throwback! A congenital ape!

"Leave me alone!" he said.

She left without a backward glance and returned to the ruins. But she reappeared a few minutes later carrying the goatskin bag. She had a handful of leaves that she had plucked from the jungle of garden, and she carefully placed them on the grass beside him. Then she took out a knife. Keen and sharp, its blade flashed in the sun and he thought she was going to stab him. But she hacked away the long leather straps of her shoulder bag.

"If you bind these leaves to your leg, it will stop the festering," she said. "Will you do it, or shall I?"

Her white eyes met Simon's in a kind of challenge. He did not want her touching him but finally he nodded. Pale hairy fingers made a compress of leaves, a pad from a white linen handkerchief, bound his leg with leather thongs, and fastened the knot. The hood of her gown that had been hiding her face slipped to reveal the snow-white fur of her countenance, her primate features. Her face was not deformed in any way, no degeneration of bone structure. It was the white animal fur that repelled him and made her a simian thing. Mutation was cruel, and so was Simon. His dislike of her actually showed, and he offered her no thanks.

The ape girl shrugged, picked up her things, and went back to her digging. He could hear the hack of her pick and shovel in the dark interior of the ruined building. Appearances ought not to matter. There were mutants everywhere, Harris had said, and they were no less human than the people in the bunker. Simon went to apologize, limped along the track toward the house. Flies were already feeding on the body of the dog, and the heat of the day was building up. Stepping from sunlight into shadow, he had to wait for his eyes to grow accustomed, and she was just a vague white shape crouching below a fallen roof beam. But then he noticed the forked stick held in her hand, its slow steady motion above the cleared floor space before it jerked and twisted and she laid it down and once more started to dig.

Simon watched her curiously. Carefully she unearthed the bones of a skeletal hand, plucked a gold ring from its finger, and placed it in her bag. Then she picked up the stick again. A few quick jerks and she unearthed the other hand, retrieved a diamond dress ring and a gold bracelet hanging with charms.

"Grave robbing!" Simon said in disgust.

"Jewels are no good to the dead," she said.

"I suppose you sell them?"

"Sell?" she questioned. "What's that? I give them to the artisans at Timberley."

"And what do they give you in return?"

"Nothing," she said. "Why should they?"

She seemed not to have heard of trade or barter, although back at the bunker they had been trading with outsiders for years. Every fleece, every goatskin, every scrap of metal was loaded annually into the one remaining army truck, driven to the settlements at Watchet or Sedgemoor, and exchanged for food. But now they had run out of gasoline, just as they had run out of basic chemicals for the culture tanks. There were no more cloned vegetables. The soil in the glass-house area was exhausted, and the land around the bunker failed to grow. They were beginning to know the meaning of starvation and suffering. They were all half naked and undernourished—children with rickets, adults with scurvy, old people dying of hypothermia when the winter set in. It was cold underground and often dark, and there were no more spare parts to keep the electric generators going. Their only chance of surviving was to move outside. And whatever Simon thought, he could not insult a girl with a fistful of gold from whose people Harris had come to beg.

He chewed his lip.

And was bound to accept what she did.

"You need a geiger counter," he said.

"I already have one," she replied.

"I could trade you a battery-powered model."

She picked up the stick.

"This one is mind powered," she told him. "It can find whatever I want it to find, whatever we need— wood, clay, or water, gold or glass, old bones, and buried scrap metal. What can yours do?"

Simon stared at her. The way she spoke of her mental powers made him uneasy. Maybe she was not subhuman and primitive. Maybe she was superhuman, her mind gone way beyond his. Yet he dismissed the thought. It was instinct, he reasoned. Some uncanny instinct that enabled her to home in on things. Powers like that were nothing new. Records of prewar society showed that many people had claimed to possess them. There was even a name for it, which Simon failed to remember.

"Psychic," said the girl, as if she had read his mind. "I'm a water diviner, among other things, and my name is Laura. You had no need to shoot that dog, you know. I could have controlled it. My mind is stronger than an animal's mind. Stronger than yours too."

Simon sat on the crumbling edge of the windowsill. There was a throbbing pain in his leg.

He did not believe what she told him.

Laura laughed teasingly.

"Once people believed that a nuclear holocaust would never happen," she said.

ㅇㅇㅇ

Simon limped along the track behind the others. He carried a backpack of camping gear, and the mid-morning sun made him sweat inside his suit. Just for a moment he wished he were like Laura, stripped to a simple shift, with the heavy hooded gown stowed away in her goatskin bag, her limbs bare and her long fair hair blowing in the wind. The fine albino fur covered her completely, but it also protected her. Laura had nothing to fear from the ultraviolet light.

Harris and Sowerby seemed to accept what she was, or perhaps they no longer noticed. They had had dealings with mutants before and grown used to it. Usually, Sowerby told Simon, mutant people did not remove their robes, the cowled hoods that concealed their deformities. But Laura walked as if she were proud of it.

Simon was too far behind to hear what they talked of. Standing stones, probably. Sowerby was obsessed with standing stones. He was a qualified cartographer, and the maps in the bunker were years out of date. There had been no aerial surveys in Simon's lifetime.

Landmarks had vanished. The major areas of inhabitation had shifted, and only the standing stones remained, visually linking the empty distances. What their purpose was, and why they had been restored, was something Sowerby had always wanted to know.

Sowerby belonged to a generation of academics, hot on theory but pretty useless when it came to practical know-how. Like Grandfather Harnden, Simon's mother had always warned them what would happen. They were dinosaurs in a bunker, not knowing how to knit or sew, spin or weave, make planks from tree trunks, carpenter wood, or make a cart wheel. Nobody could use a hammer or anvil, fashion metal, pulp paper, or manufacture decent shoes. Everything they did was just a bungling attempt, and work on the land and animal husbandry were looked on as punishment duty.

They had clung too long to prewar attitudes and old ideals, thinking they were some kind of elite. All their energies had gone into keeping up civilized standards. They still dreamed of restoring the country to what it had been. And Simon himself had grown up convinced that he was superior to the weavers and crofters and fishermen who dwelled in the outside communities. He had actually believed that academic education and an ability to do advanced calculus placed him above them. But not anymore. A mutant girl had ended all that, and all his illusions were gone.

Fearless and free in the sun that would burn him, Laura strode across the hill. She believed that the nuclear war had marked not the ending of civilization, but the beginning. She believed she had been born into a better world than the one that was gone, that her people were better people. She saw Simon as a remnant of the old evil and believed that *she* was superior to *him*.

It was humiliating, because in a way it was true. They had achieved nothing in the bunker that could prove her wrong. She was well clothed, well fed, secure in her way of life with her primitive religious beliefs and her geiger-counter mind. For her, reality was good and she had no need to dream of a better world. And Simon was as well schooled as Sowerby and Harris, in theory, but he could do damn little in practice.

"We can make bricks," Laura had boasted.

"I suppose you use them for building hovels?" Simon had asked.

"We build cathedrals," she replied.

Simon hated her for that. Perhaps it was automatic. Her appearance alone made her different from him, and human beings had always feared and hated anyone who was different. Simon saw himself as normal, Laura as abnormal. He was human, she was a mutant. But her kind had everything, his kind nothing, and he resented it. Blood ran down his leg and soaked his moccasin as she stopped and looked back.

"Are you all right, Simon?" called Harris.

"Want us to chairlift you?" Sowerby asked.

"I'm not a cripple!" Simon shouted.

And Laura laughed.

They were already halfway down the hill when Simon reached the top. The valley was below him, blurred by plastic and indistinct. He stood with his back to the sun and raised his visor, drew in his breath. It was an incredible sight. Fields of oats and barley rippled in the wind, and there were trees like he had never seen before, towers of silvery leaves swaying and sighing. Birds sang and bean flowers smelled sweet, and woods grew on the hills beyond. Yet Simon hardly saw all that. It was just a setting for the great building that dominated everything.

This was not the place his mother had visited, a village of tin-roofed shacks and battered glass houses. The building Simon was seeing was not even western in design. It reminded him of a Tibetan monastery he had once viewed on the computer video screen before the electronics broke down. Sheer walls rose several stories high, smooth and plastered and colored dusky yellow. Rows of tiny windows watched him like eyes, and the slate roofs shone silver in the light. It was built in a square enclosing a vast central courtyard, and on each side an archway led in beneath its walls. East, west, south, and north, four tracks led away from it.

North beyond the building the stream had been dammed, making a small lake where wild ducks nested in the reed beds and naked children swam. Willow trees grew on its banks and sluice gates let out the water. The stream flowed on through pale meadows where cattle grazed, past hay barns and milking barns and a flour mill where a great wheel turned, and on again past the sewage beds where the arms of sprinklers slowly revolved.

These people had thought of everything. Not the technological revolution dreamed of in the bunker, but a way of life that was simpler and more wholesome, age-old methods that were tried and tested and seen to work. They had no need for dreams of underground air-conditioned cities, subway tunnels where solar-powered trains linked bunker to bunker, synthetic food production, or eventual colonization of worlds around other suns. They did not need qualified architects, nutrition experts, genetic engineers, army personnel-training plans, military supervision, or administration by a central government. They had managed without, flourished, and survived. And not only was this place beautiful, it was functional as well.

Simon's head started to spin and his vision darkened. He had been traveling for three days and had hardly eaten anything since they had left the bunker. Comparisons appalled him. He saw an alien fortress in an English valley, a girl walking free in the sunlight, a community that lived and thrived on the harsh outer surface of the world where he could have no place. He thought of crumbling concrete, dark decaying passageways, and broken-down machinery. His mother was right. They were dinosaurs in a bunker. They could not live beneath the sun that whirled and spun and blazed its yellow light. Extinction stared him in the face as the world turned black and Simon hit the dust.

◦◦◦

Simon hardly remembered arriving at the settlement. It was just an impression of yellow outside walls and dark inside shade, a feeling of relief when someone stripped him of his suit. He saw vague white faces. Heard a babble of indistinct voices before he went spinning away through the black empty spaces of unconsciousness. Someone made him drink . . . icy water from an earthenware cup. His leg hurt like hell, and he was lying on a scrubbed table with a straw pallet under his head, in a room that was whitewashed and cool. Harris and Sowerby were standing in the doorway. He could see the courtyard beyond them, flowering baskets hanging from the cloistered walkway, the shaded overhang of the upper floors, and a covered well with a pool of sunlit water in the middle.

"We're moving on," Harris was saying. "Thanks for the meal. You've been most helpful."

"We'll look after Simon," Laura said.

"Okay," said Harris. "Tell him we'll call for him on the way back."

Simon went to sit up.

A fast hand held him down.

And Laura returned to him.

"Lie still! You'll disturb the pins!" she said.

Simon remembered then. He had not been unconscious all the time. He remembered Laura telling him that someone called Johnson had taken the pins from the offices of a practicing acupuncturist who had died in the holocaust, learned how to use them from instruction manuals, and passed the knowledge on. Now Lilith was using them on Simon to block the neuronal pathways. She was going to suture the gash in his leg and he would not feel pain. But he would not be able to walk either, at least not well enough to keep up with Harris and Sowerby.

"Enjoy yourself, Simon," Harris told him.

And Lilith laughed.

It was a mad laugh, guttural and imbecilic, the sound of a mute woman for whom Laura translated. Lilith too was a mutant, an aging hairy albino with white stringy locks and those same white eyes. Her smile showed a mouthful of rotting teeth, and black pinprick pupils led deep into her mind. There was something about her Simon did not like, a look of gloating satisfaction, like a prophetess seeing in him the truth of her own predictions. Fear shot through the nerves of his stomach as he saw the catgut thread and needle in her hand.

Suddenly he was screaming "Don't let her touch me!" Struggling like a wild thing to be off that operating table. He forgot about the four hundred people in the government bunker who needed to be rehoused. He forgot about survival being dependent on outsiders. He only knew he was not being operated on by a witch doctor, or left behind with a load of goddamn apes! His language was rude and abusive, completely irrational. Diplomatically Harris acted in the only way he could. A hard right fist to Simon's jaw sent him spinning away into a black oblivion.

When he awoke, he had been moved to another room—a whitewashed cell with a small window set high in the outer wall. Or maybe it only seemed high because his bed was a mattress on the floor. From the lateness of the light he guessed it was evening, although he was not sure if it was today or tomorrow, or how long he had slept.

He turned his head. A person was seated on a stool by the door, a shrunken, unmoving human figure, the most hideous creature he had ever seen. An old gray dress informed him she was female, and her mouth sagged open as she slept, showing toothless gums. Her hair was gone and her scalp was a mass of festering sores. Red burning skin, puckered and wrinkled, made up her face. She was bones covered by flesh, rotting away even as he watched her.

Simon could not have guessed her age, but Grandfather Harnden had been almost ninety when he died and he had never looked like that. This aged crone must have lived right through it, the nuclear war and the radioactive fallout, the fire and the dust.

Naked beneath the blanket, Simon turned away his head, unable to look at her, unable to escape, trapped with her in the prison room as the twilight deepened and the evening grew chill. He could hear voices in the rest of the building, far away and muffled by walls, but he had never experienced such total isolation. It was as if he were the only human being left alive, and the thing by the doorway belonged to some other species. Then the door quietly opened.

"I've brought you some soup," said Laura.

Almost eagerly Simon turned to face her. Her simian appearance no longer mattered. She was someone he knew, young and beautiful, compared to that festering old woman. His stomach was hollow with hunger, but Laura had not been speaking to him. He watched as she placed the dish and spoon in the old woman's hands. Shriveled fingers gripped like a baby's, and Laura guided the spoon to her mouth. Simon realized then that she was blind, and from across the room the white eyes of the mutant girl met his own. He could actually feel the pity, not for the dying creature she was feeding, but for him.

"This is my grandmother," she said fondly. "She is blind Kate now, but she taught us how to see things clearly . . . who we are and how we came to be."

"God looked on the earth and saw it was wicked," the old woman muttered. "That men had corrupted His ways with their evil and violence, and He decided to destroy them." She laid down her spoon. Her clawed hands gripped at Laura's arm. "Is he awake?" she asked.

"He's awake," Laura confirmed.

"Ask him," said blind Kate. "Ask him if he knows them."

"It was thirty-five years ago," Laura objected. "Simon was not even born then, and your kind of people seldom live very long."

"I have," blind Kate retorted.

"You had a reason to," Laura said. "And not everyone has your willpower."

The old woman sighed and went back to her spooning.

Soup dribbled from her chin as Simon watched.

"Do you want something to eat?" Laura asked him.

"Yes," Simon said sourly. "And where are my clothes?"

"We washed them and they fell to pieces. I'll bring you some new ones in the morning. I didn't expect to find you awake. Aunt Lilith gave you a sleeping draft, and we thought you would sleep through the night."

"She had no right to do that!" Simon said angrily.

Blind Kate waved her spoon.

"*He* talked like that," she said. "That Colonel Allison who came from the government in Avon. He talked about rights. He said we had no right to our own cattle and tried to steal them. It was the day your mother was born, Laura, and we named her after him. Johnson always said they would be back. But they haven't come to steal this time, oh no. They have come to beg. And we give, of course, just as we always do."

Simon sat up.

His voice was sharp.

"What's she talking about?"

"Sometimes," said Laura, "she gets confused."

"I've survived for more than sixty years," blind Kate went on. "Sarah said I was meant to, but I knew it anyway. I thought she was Sarah come back . . . Sarah and my father and Colonel Allison. But she wasn't Sarah. She had another name. Amelia, I think it was, Amelia Harnden, and she was my sister too. Ask him if he knows her."

"It was too long ago," Laura repeated.

"Ask him," blind Kate insisted.

White eyes turned to Simon.

"Do you?" Laura asked.

"No," he said.

But he did. The name was not Amelia—it was Ophelia. She had married Wayne Allison and was Simon's mother. This was the place she had talked of. This was the place she had visited with Grandfather Harnden and Grandpop Allison all those years ago. Blind Kate was his mother's sister, and Laura was a cousin. He was actually related to them, cousin to a mutant. Simon was not sure how he felt—sort of sick and revolted. It was a relationship he could never accept, never admit, not even to himself.

ooo

Simon did not sleep too well during the night. His thoughts plagued him, and the strong cheese he had eaten for supper gave him indigestion. His leg ached uncomfortably. He was accustomed to silence and absolute darkness, but here the moonlight was as bright as day. Night birds screamed and dogs howled on the surrounding hills, and Lilith came creeping into his room to check on him. She made incomprehensible guttural noises that were meant to soothe but instead served to alarm him, and examined his injured leg by candlelight. No blood showed through the linen dressings, so she smiled her gloating smile and went away.

The flax plants had come from Ireland, Laura had told him during supper, and now they grew them locally at another settlement, acres of blue flowers in a nearby valley. Soon her people would have summer clothes as well as winter ones, she said. It was one more accomplishment she had to boast about, and one more reason for Simon to hate her. But he was not afraid of her, not in the way he was afraid of Lilith. She was the hag out of fairy tales that Grandfather Harnden had told him as a child, a wise woman weaving spells and brewing sleeping drafts, the archetypal witch in the midnight darkness. When she came to his room a second time, he looked at her in dread.

But it was Laura who came with the morning, smiling to see him, bringing him clothes to wear and a wooden crutch to help him walk. Gooseflesh prickled his skin as he dressed in a long-sleeved shirt of creamy wool, a short brown tunic, brown knitted ankle socks, and leather sandals with carved buckles of bone. He had never worn clothes like that before. Each garment seemed like a work of art, fine and comfortable. He needed a mirror to admire them, and opened the door to find Laura waiting outside—her face in the sunlight white and furry, his cousin, an ape. Simon leaned on the crutch and she moved to help him, an ape girl touching his arm. He shook her away.

"I can manage!" he said violently.

Laura shrugged, and he followed her along the balcony. Above and around him the building was coming awake, doors being opened to let in the morning light. Every family had its own apartment, Laura told him, but everything else was done communally. Voices of children and adults sounded on the upper levels, but the well of the courtyard below was silent and empty, dark with shadow. Walls towered over him as Simon clung to the railings and descended the stairs.

Laura waited for him at the bottom in the shade of the overhang, pale and wraithlike in her long white gown. Above her head a basket of flowers shivered in the draft from the western archway, their glorious colors dampened with dew. He could see looms and spinning wheels in the workshop behind her, and a crude metal printing press in another. Laura pointed.

"The washroom's over there," she said. "If you go now, no one will see you."

"Why should I care who sees me?" Simon asked huffily.

"No one likes being stared at," Laura replied.

Simon supposed they were bound to stare because he was a stranger, but he discovered later that that was not the reason. He was seated in the dining hall at one of the long wooden tables. Except for the cooks at the far end serving hot chicory coffee, whole-meal rolls, and scrambled eggs, the room had been empty when he and Laura entered it. He was used to communal eating, so he had taken no notice when the people started filing in . . . not until the noise and whispering stopped.

Everyone was staring at him in complete silence, men, women, and children—and every one of them a mutant. Simon stared back at them in shock and horror—several hundred furry albinos with blank white eyes and black pinprick pupils taking note of him . . . his bare legs, his smooth skin, brown eyes, and black curling hair. It was *he* who was different!

"What's that, Mommy?" one small child asked.

Laura rose to her feet.

"This is Simon," she announced. "He has come to stay with us. I hope we'll all welcome him and do our best to make him happy."

Mutant men nodded and smiled.

Mutant women glanced and whispered.

Mutant children asked questions.

And the answers carried.

"No dear, he isn't an animal."

"He's like blind Kate was when she was young."

"Once upon a time all people looked like him."

"They were all bald skinned."

"No darling, he isn't dangerous, not to us."

"Yes, they *did* kill each other."

"But there's not many left of them now."

"And they're not too clever at staying alive."

"That's why some of them are coming to live with us."

"We have to look after them, you see?"

"And you must always be kind to him."

"He can't help what he is."

A lump of bread stuck in Simon's throat, a morsel of their pity that threatened to choke him. He wanted to lash out at them, scream at them, tell them they were wrong. All over England, in every government bunker, there were communities of people who were just like him . . . except that he was not sure about that. The communications system had broken down years ago, and they had lost contact. It might be true. He might be a member of a dying breed. But if it was true, and the human race as Simon saw it really was on the verge of extinction, one thing Simon knew for certain . . . he did not want a load of hairy mutants offering him pity!

He crammed the remains of his whole-meal roll into his mouth, picked up his crutch, and walked out. He had to get away from them, those white eyes and the eerie minds behind them. He had to get away from this place. He was not ending up like blind Kate being spoon-fed on sympathy and pap! He left by the northern archway and entered the sun, felt it cruel and burning on the backs of his legs and neck. His flesh would fry before he had traveled a couple of miles. He limped along the track toward the dammed-up stream, seeking the shade of the willow trees, and Laura came running behind.

"Leave me alone!" Simon howled.

"I'm sorry," she said. "Sorry for what happened in there. I did try to warn you, but the children were bound to ask questions. We never meant you to be upset."

"Stuff your apologies!" said Simon.

"What else do you want me to say?" she asked wildly. "Would you rather we hated you? Threw stones at you? Spat in your face?"

"At least it would be understandable!"

"Why would it?"

"Because we're the ones who made you what you are!"

Laura stared at him.

"There's nothing wrong with the way we are," she said levelly. "And violence is incompatible with intelligence. I don't understand why you're behaving like this. We're doing our best. We're trying to make you feel at home here. If you wanted to eat alone, you should have said so. You're not obliged to mix with us. We know what you and your people have been through. Harris told us that. We're not heartless. We've agreed to take in as many of you as we can. So what's wrong, Simon? We're willing to give you everything you need. What more can we do?"

Simon closed his eyes. Sunlight and shade from the willow leaves flickered on his face, and her words hurt like cruelty, like nails being driven home, a slow crucifixion. They in the bunkers had never cared what happened to the outsiders, so why should Laura care about him? Why should she give? Share? Offer? Everything she had?

"Can't you see?" he groaned.

She sighed.

"Obviously I can't," she said. "Lilith says our eyes are different from yours. We see blue silver shining on a rainbow land. We see the veils of ultraviolet light, its shifting intensities. We see the damaged sky. Where things will grow and where they will never grow beneath it. It's bad land around your bunker, I expect. And we see you, Simon. Electrical auras around all living things, white and gold and glowing, but yours is dark and depressing and I don't know what to say or how to help you."

Simon clenched his fists.

Laura was either innocent or stupid.

And he did not believe in auras.

"You've already said it!" Simon said bitterly. "If you're all right then there's obviously something wrong with me! I'm not only sick . . . I'm a freak! And there's only one way you can help me. Bug off and leave me alone!"

∘∘∘

Simon sat in the shade of the willow trees. Sunlight reflected on the surface of the water and the green woods brooded on the hills beyond. He could hear the sounds of the settlement behind him, a rattle of butter churns and women's laughter. Downstream the mill wheel was turning. Cows chewed their cuds in the sleepy morning pastures, and men worked in the bean fields up the valley. Seen from a distance, pale skinned and human in shape, they looked no different from himself.

It was he who was a congenital freak, genetically isolated, unable to join them in the merciless light of the sun. Without the white protective suit, Simon was useless. His skin would burn and blister, form weeping sores that were slow to heal, that turned into skin cancer and finally killed. If he wished to escape from this place, he would have to travel at night, or not travel at all. The tree shadows trapped him and loneliness plagued him like the flies.

Mutants came and went along the dusty track between the outbuildings and the settlement. Small children played in the shallows at the other end of the lake. Nobody approached him. He supposed Laura had warned them away. His behavior so far had not been exactly friendly. He was moody and vicious, dangerous if provoked, like a trapped animal. He slapped at the flies that buzzed around his eyes, stripped off the warm woollen shirt, and swilled his face in the water. Reflections settled and stilled. A gong sounded and the children went away. The loneliness intensified with the heat, and Simon wished he had never set out with Harris and Sowerby.

Back in the bunker they still had hope. They thought if they threw in their lot with the outsiders, they would go on surviving. And maybe they would, an endangered species kept by the mutants like animals in a zoo, incapable of fending for themselves. In the bunker they saw it as a solution, but there *was* no solution. Out here in the stark hot land there was no future for the likes of him, just life without dignity and total dependence.

It was not Laura's fault. She had offered him charity and it was not her fault he could not accept. Violence was incompatible with intelligence, Laura had said, and in this postnuclear world it had no place. They should have listened to the warning cries of the peace protesters before the war. In the government bunker they should have listened to Grandfather Harnden, although even then it had been too late.

All her life Grandmother Erica had worked in the food laboratories. All her life Ophelia had peered at chromosomes down a microscope, while Sowerby messed around with his maps and Harris struggled to keep the generator running. Not one of them had faced the reality. They should have known resources were finite, that prewar supplies of gasoline, raw chemicals, and component parts were bound to run out. They should have known that if they did not adapt to changed environmental conditions, they were doomed to die out. They had sacrificed their children's futures for a technological breakthrough that had never happened, left Simon to face what they could not . . . that mutants would inherit the earth.

Homo sapiens! The name itself was an irony. They had not been wise at all, but incredibly stupid—stupid enough to murder the environment on which they were dependent. Yet, thinking of himself, Simon knew he was not stupid, nor had he ever killed anything, except for the dog. It was only in comparison to Laura that he appeared mentally deficient and emotionally unstable. As Neanderthal man had been to *Homo sapiens*, so he was to her . . . a lower species.

He heard a scuff of footsteps in the dust behind him and turned his head. Blind Kate was standing on the shadow line. She carried a wicker basket and was leaning on a walking stick. A straw hat shaded her ravaged face from the sun, but her arms were exposed, patches of raw red skin forming among the festering sores. Blue faded eyes stared sightlessly across the distances. Her dying voice called his name, and called again when he did not answer her.

Simon held his breath, watched and waited to see what she would do. She was his aunt, his own mother's sister, but he could not bring himself to acknowledge her. Nor did he want her near him. What she was was what he dreaded most of all, an image of his own future, an ailing pathetic thing. She shuffled toward him and put down the basket. Her breath rattled and she shouted.

"I know you're there! You didn't want my Laura! But she sent this for you! It's green-salad sandwiches, strawberries and cream, cold mint tea, and a caftan to keep off the sun. You come and get it! I know you're there."

From the dry grass at her feet Simon stared up at her. Emotions tore at him and he wanted to scream. He did not want their gifts . . . strawberries and cream and a fancy caftan. He would rather fry and starve than accept. But blind Kate held it toward him, cool white linen with a loose hood. Unseeing eyes looked directly at him, as if she knew he was there. Her lips twisted in scorn.

"Give it, she told me. Give it to him. And all this morning was spent in making it. And she picked the strawberries herself. That's how we taught her. We have no right to keep things to ourselves. What others need, Laura will give, if she can. That's how we taught them all. They must be better people, Johnson said. Better than us. And so they are. True to her kind, my Laura is, and better than you. They are all better than you. You only know how to take, don't you? Take for yourself, not give and receive. I remember, my fine young man. I remember the likes of you!"

Simon bit his lip.

Blind Kate had mothered mutants, fostered a new way of life, but she had not forgotten how to hurt. Laura inflicted cruelty by kindness, not even knowing, but blind Kate chose her words and used them like knives, truth cutting into him, paying him back for his nastiness to the granddaughter she loved. There was nothing pathetic about blind Kate now. She was the originator of a settlement, a survivor against all odds, revered and respected.

A gobbet of her saliva smacked on the dusty grass beside him. "Worthless!" she said. "Yes, we were most of us worthless, not knowing how to cherish this earth and each other! We allowed no wickedness here, Johnson and I. But you have learned nothing, hiding away in your bunker. Think to despise her, don't you? Think yourself better than she? But you'll learn the truth of it yet, my boy. You'll learn!"

Simon reached for the caftan and clutched it to his chest. It was soft and beautiful, a gift from a girl who was better than both of them. He would put it on when blind Kate was gone and leave this place.

ooo

The caftan billowed in the hot summer wind as Simon crossed the dam, hung in graceful folds and swished around his ankles when he entered the wood. It did something for him, changed his whole personality, set him free from the galling humiliation of his own humanity. He was free to walk among the silences of trees and actually enjoy himself. He saw a colony of tiny birds feeding on the blight that dropped from the high branches. He saw day moths fluttering in the shafts of yellow light. Ferns and foxgloves grew amid the undergrowth, and he could smell the fragrance of the air. White protective suits and plastic visors had cut him off from all of this, but the caftan was different.

It let him become a part of the life that was all around him, and extinction seemed a thing of the past.

The path ascended steeply to the top of the hill, and the stitches in his leg pulled uncomfortably. But he had left his crutch on the grass, along with the woollen undershirt and the empty basket, and he was not going back. He climbed a stile in the wall that bordered the plantation, emerged onto empty moorland in the wind and sun, and pulled up his hood. Sheep grazed on the gold gorse hills before him, and the valley was behind him and below, sheened with sunlight, the great yellow building diminished by height, grown small among its surrounding fields.

Seen from above, it was not so impressive—just a square-built kibbutz, housing a simple rural community. Laura believed that mutation was an evolutionary step forward, but maybe it was not. He saw no evidence of an advanced society. Quite the reverse. It was simplistic and retrogressive, almost medieval. Technologically, mutants were centuries behind the people who lived in the government bunker.

Simon felt his confidence restored. Maybe Laura was a nicer person than he, but her life-style was archaic. As a species, the mutants faced stagnation. They had no drive, no ambitions, no go-ahead ideas. Simple agricultural survival was not enough, and Laura had nothing to brag about, no more than he.

He brushed leaf mold and pine needles from his caftan and headed out across the moors, limping toward a group of standing stones he saw on the far skyline. He knew Harris and Sowerby had planned to go north and work their way west through the various communities, so he reasoned that if he went west and worked his way north he was bound to meet up with them. West was where the standing stones were, the way the wind came, untempered across the open empty spaces and tearing at his hood. He had to hang on to it and could feel the sun's rays burning the back of his hand.

The stones were farther than he thought. He had to detour around vast areas of bog. His leg hurt and it was early evening before he reached them. He sheltered from the wind and sun in the lee of a giant upright. A spot of bright blood showed through the bandages, and he was beginning to feel hungry again. He looked for the next settlement, but only a church tower showed above the western horizon.

Simon had seen no evidence of organized religion among Laura's people, but he reasoned that where there was a church there was bound to be a village. He walked slowly toward it, picking bilberries as he went. He could survive forever out on these moors on the rich dark berries and water from the stony streams. The sun was already setting when he knelt to drink, drained of heat and dazzling his eyes. He did not know what made him glance around . . . a sensing perhaps.

The dogs were low on their bellies, pack hunting, fanning out through the gorse and heather. Simon ran, great limping strides, not caring about the gash in his leg, not caring about anything except the fear that drove him. He had no rifle, no defense. His only hope was to outrun them, reach the church and seek sanctuary inside. But the distance was almost a mile, and he knew he would never make it.

The plane seemed to fly from the sun, a snow-white glider with wings gleaming golden in the light, drifting down the thermals of windy air and dipping toward him. Lower it came, and lower, making its turn, whistling in from the northern hills, skimming the surface of the land, bending heather and grasses in a rush of speed. It passed directly behind him, between himself and the dogs, giving him space.

Simon did not stop to watch; he went on running. And the plane stayed with him, circling and dropping, its great white presence warding off the attack. With its every approach the dogs fell back, snarled, and waited as Simon ran on. The caftan billowed. The wind whipped off his hood and the low sun burned his face, but he could not stop. He ran until his lungs were bursting, and blood soaked through the bandages, ran down his leg, and stained the earth with his scent. The dogs would not give up, but he made it to the church ahead of them as the white plane circled and dropped for one last time.

Simon entered the tower. The door had fallen inward, and maybe he should have gone for the main body of the church, but it was too late now. He skidded to a halt among a mess of mortar and bird droppings, moldering hymn books, and rotting shelves. Inside, it was almost too dark to see, and the door leading into the nave was locked. Simon spun around. He could just make out the shape of a vestry chest standing in the corner. It was solid oak, but his brute strength shifted it and he hauled it across the gap of the doorway. He tore at the fallen shelves that had once held hymn books, tried to wedge them on top, a crisscross barricade that refused to stay in place. He saw the glider heading away into the sunset. He saw white fangs and milky eyes as one dog gathered itself to spring; he grabbed a fallen spar and lashed as it leaped.

The dog howled and fell backward, turned tail, and ran as another took its place. Again Simon lashed, a blow to its head that laid it temporarily unconscious. The other dogs circled outside among grass and gravestones. He knew they would not go away. They would stay there all night if they had to, work out a coordinated attack. He needed to build the barricade higher, and there was a board in the corner, leaning against the wall where the vestry chest had been. Away from the weather it had been preserved. Gold lettering on black paint told the times of weekly services. Saint Andrew's Rushfield, the church was called. Keeping an eye on the space of the doorway, Simon dragged it across the room, heaved it on top of the chest. It completely blocked the doorway apart from a twelve-inch gap at the top. He used the weight of his body to hold it in place and was finally safe.

Simon sat in the almost total darkness, trembling in every limb, not daring to move. The board was hard and his shoulder was jammed against it, but he knew it would hold as long as he himself did not slacken. Movement was difficult, and he was already feeling sick from exertion, and when he touched the bandage on his leg it was sodden with blood, warm and sticky on his fingers, pumping more with every heartbeat. He had torn open the stitches and was likely to bleed to death.

He must have been mad to leave the settlement! Mad to walk the hills without a rifle! In this new world grown from the dust of war, dogs had always been a danger. And there was a limit to how long he could hole up here in this crumbling tower without food or

water. Dogs scrabbled at the inner door that led through
to the nave of the church. Suppose, while they were
in there, he made a run for it?

He tried to remember what he had seen outside. No
village or settlement, just gravestones and a derelict
vicarage, a few ruined cottages and a track leading
downhill into a tangled valley with a river at the bottom. He tried to remember Sowerby's map. If that
was the river Wye he had seen below, then there were
no settlements nearby. They were all to the north and
he was too far west, outside the area Harris and Sowerby had planned to travel. He should have turned
north at the standing stones, headed for the settlement
at Newlington. Now he could either go back the way
he had come or make for Timberley, which was somewhere down in the valley . . . a good six miles in either
direction. Simon knew he would never make it. He
was trapped in the tower and no one knew he was
there, except for the glider pilot.

Who was it could fly a glider in these parts? Mutants
had no technology, so it had to come from a government bunker—probably the headquarters of the
Special Armed Services division at Hereford. Simon
reckoned it would be morning before they could reach
him, and the following morning if they had no trucks
or gasoline. But it gave him something to hope for,
set a time scale for his imprisonment.

Dogs gnawed at the woodwork of the inner door.
Others prowled and whined around the perimeter walls.
Night birds screamed in the belfry above him as Simon
settled down to wait. It was only thirty-six hours at
most, he told himself, but every minute seemed endless.

◦◦◦

Simon was gripped by a lethargy that made him feel almost comfortable, his mind drifting between sleeping and waking, gone beyond fear or pain. His shoulder had become numb from where the signboard cut into it, but he was no longer aware of that. Then a sound in the distance caused him to listen, a nickering whinny and a heavy clopping tread, some kind of large unidentifiable animal. The dogs snarled and snapped with their teeth, whined and retreated as the creature came on toward the tower and stopped outside. He could hear the creak of leather, the jangle of metal, and the snort of its breath.

"Simon?" said Laura. "Are you in there?"

In sheer relief Simon let go. The board crashed to the floor and he saw her sitting there, Laura in the moonlight with her pale hair blowing in the wind, white robed and slender, riding a horse. He had not known horses still existed, but this one was real enough. Splotched piebald, it tossed its head and aimed a kick as the dogs approached it. Laura stroked its mane.

"This is Timms," she said. "He was given to us by Morgan's people, who live in the north of Wales. Are you all right? I got here as fast as I could."

"How did you find me?" Simon asked in astonishment.

"Tyler told us where you were."

"Who's Tyler?"

"The glider pilot. Are you going to stay in there all night, or will you come back to the settlement?"

"I'm not coming out there with those dogs," said Simon.

"I'll get rid of them," Laura said.

She slid from the horse's back. The dogs were only a few yards from her, gleaming eyes and teeth showing white in the moonlight. She turned to face them, inviting them to attack. But they kept their distance, and she raised her hand, pointed away at the midnight hills. "Go!" she said. And the dogs obeyed her, sank to their bellies and slunk away. She was stronger than they were. Stronger in her mind. And stronger than Simon, too. He got dizzy the moment he moved and collapsed on the ground.

When he came to, he was lying amid the litter on the floor. Single-handedly Laura had shifted the heavy chest from the doorway, and a candle in a jam jar shed a flickering light, gleamed in the horse's eyes outside, and showed Laura kneeling beside him with a blood-soaked dressing in her hand.

"That was stupid!" she said. "A stupid thing to do! *Why* did you do it? Why run away from us? You had only to say you wanted to leave, and we would have given you Timms, gone with you, shown you the way! You might have died if Tyler hadn't spotted you. Are we so ugly and repulsive you couldn't even bear to spend a few days with us? What's wrong with us, Simon? What's wrong with *me*?"

Simon sat with his back against the wall. There was *nothing* wrong with Laura. She was a wonderful, beautiful person. Strands of her hair were the color of moonlight, but her eyes were white and on her arms the pale fur shone with sheen. There was nothing wrong with that either, except that Simon could not accept it. He could not forget she was a mutant. He tried to explain.

"There's nothing wrong with you. It's me who's wrong. I'm prejudiced, I suppose. Human and stupid. It's in me and I can't change myself. I don't measure up to you and I never will."

"In other words you have an inferiority complex?"

"It's how you make me feel," said Simon.

"We don't mean to," said Laura. "We respect what you are, just as we respect all forms of life. You're sacred, Simon. Everything is."

"I can't buy that quasi-religious bullshit!"

"Surely it's axiomatic?" said Laura.

"Axio-what?"

"A self-evident universally accepted truth."

"Since when?"

"Since, failing to see it, your kind engineered a nuclear war and almost destroyed everything."

"That's what I mean!" Simon said furiously. "That's what it all boils down to! The sins of my fathers! I've inherited what they did, a madman on the road to extinction! I'm a member of a useless species, don't you see? I've got no future, and I've got no purpose, and I don't need you to spell it out! I know I'm useless! I've been getting the message loud and clear from the moment I met you! Well, thanks for the lesson, but I'm not staying around to have it rubbed in!"

Laura said nothing, went outside, took a compress and bandage from the saddlebag, and rebound his leg. She gave him bread and cheese, water from a leather canteen, and the woollen shirt to wear under his caftan. Then she put on her gown, blew out the candle, and waited for him to rise.

"Where do you want to go?" she asked him.

"How the hell would I know?" Simon snapped.

"I'll take you to Timberley," she decided.

"That's miles away!"

"You can ride the horse."

"I don't know *how* to ride a horse!"

"All you need to do is sit on his back," said Laura. "Surely even *you* can manage that much?"

Timms was loaded with bedrolls and blankets, standing patiently as Simon attempted to mount. But his leg felt dead, unable to support him, unable to provide the necessary thrust. Laura had to help him, slim fingers clutching his waist. And something boosted him, some huge force propelling him upward until he was suddenly sitting astride and looking down on her.

"How did you do that?" he asked in surprise.

"I eat spinach," said Laura. "Like the legendary Popeye the sailor."

"Who the hell was he?" Simon asked.

Laura caught hold of the rein and led Timms from the churchyard as Simon swayed and steadied himself, gripped with his knees and clung to the saddle. He expected to take the track to the valley, but instead they stayed on the high ground, and the moon on the river made a silver ribbon in the darkness below. Trees shivered on the wooded slopes, unreal and glittering, like the landscape of a dream. It had all become dream-like, and a girl with white-gold hair was leading him on through timeless distances under the vast expanse of starry sky in a world he did not know.

The moon sank behind them. Simon was sagging with tiredness, and his backside ached from riding before Laura suddenly stopped. He raised his head and saw a towering cromlech on the edge of a black abyss. Left and right a pathway wandered along the earth-bank borders between England and Wales, scuffed smooth by the feet of ages—old and ghost haunted in Simon's imagination. And the land fell away, hundreds of feet to the river below at the pitch-black ending of the world.

"They call this place the Devil's Pulpit," Laura said, as she helped him dismount. "We'll camp here 'til morning. I don't want Timms to break his leg."

And Simon was too weary to argue.

⚬⚬⚬

On a bed of heather with a blanket to cover him, Simon slept soundly and awoke with a start. He could smell smoke, see fire, and twigs from the dead trees crackled as Laura held out her hands to the blaze. The surrounding darkness was intensified, moonless and still in the black hour before morning. A small wind whined around the Devil's Pulpit, and the air was as cold as ice. Simon shivered, draped the blanket around his shoulder, and went to crouch by the fire. Laura added more wood.

"It will be light soon," she said. "Then we can move on."

"We didn't need to stop here in the first place," Simon muttered.

"You'd had enough," Laura stated. "And I wasn't leading Timms over the edge in the dark."

"You knew it was there, so why come this way?"

"I wanted to show you."

"Show me what?"

"The view," said Laura.

"You've brought me all this way to look at the blasted view? I suppose it didn't occur to you I could lose my leg if I don't get it seen to?"

"If you lose your leg it's your own fault," Laura retorted. "You shouldn't have set out on your own in the first place. And criticizing me won't make you any less stupid! So you may as well go back to sleep!"

"You can't give me orders!" Simon said angrily. "I'll do what I please! Go where I like, when I like, not when you say so! I'll go to Timberley on my flipping own!"

"I'll tell them to expect you," Laura said sweetly.

"Without a radio or telephone you can't tell anyone anything!" Simon said scornfully.

"Can't I?"

He stared at her, sensing the significance.

She was contradicting him.

Hinting at something that was not rational.

"How did that glider pilot tell you where to find me?" Simon inquired casually. "He didn't land at the settlement. He headed west in the opposite direction."

Laura smashed a broken branch and cast the dry wood chunks upon the fire. The flames leaped higher, coloring the whites of her eyes. Orange sheen danced on the fur of her face, showed scarlet on her hands as she once more spread them to warm.

"We use telepathy," she said.

"You what?"

"The communication of direct thought."

Simon sat back. Maybe he had sensed it right from the beginning, powers such as he had never imagined, dangerous and inhuman. Maybe that was why he had run, not wanting to face the full meaning of mutation. He remembered Lilith's black pinprick pupils drilling into him. He remembered the terror of her smile. Across the scarlet-red burning of the flames his eyes met Laura's, and this time there was no escape. She was about to tell him everything.

"Can you read my mind?" he asked.

She shook her head.

"Sometimes I can feel what you're thinking, but not often. If I could have read your mind, we wouldn't have needed Tyler to go looking for you. You have a closed mind mostly, like the rest of your kind."

"I guess Tyler is also a mutant?"

"We all are," Laura said simply.

Simon nodded grimly. Apart from blind Kate there were none of his kind left living outside, and the white-winged glider had had nothing to do with the government bunker. He had thought at the time there was something odd about it. Now he realized what that something was. No unpowered aircraft could fly like that, skim across the surface and rise using wind power alone. And what had provided the initial lift?

"Who flies the tow plane?" Simon asked.

"What tow plane?" said Laura.

"You need a tow plane to get a glider airborne."

"They use the wind off Tressilic Beacon."

"That's aerodynamically impossible."

"I don't understand."

"Where's your initial velocity? Where's your thrust?

That's not a hang glider. You've got to have power to take off."

"P.K." said Laura.

"What's that?"

"Psychokinetic energy. Mind over matter. The levitation principle. What else can we use? How else could we raise the standing stones, or build our settlements? How else could I have lifted you onto Timms' back?"

Simon closed his eyes. Black and crimson, the firelight flickered on his closed eyelids, and Laura's voice seemed to come from far away, from the distances of the future or the past. Mental powers were nothing new, she said. They had been around since the dawn of time. Probably, in the beginning, everyone had possessed them and known how to use them. Like instinct, they were necessary for survival in a world without cranes, or telephones, jet engines, submachine guns, antibiotics, and geological instruments. But the old intuitive ways of knowing and doing things had been pushed to the back of human minds, passed over in favor of logical explanations, conscious understanding, and clever machines. They had survived only dimly in memories of magic and myth. But radiation from the nuclear war and an increase in ultraviolet light had caused genetic changes, changes which were not just physical but mental as well. Maybe mutants *were* a throwback to earlier stages of human development, but more likely they were the inheritors of all the stages of evolution.

Simon struggled to accept what she was saying, the enormity of it, the huge implications. What kind of terrifying elemental force charged the neuronal circuits of the mutant brain? Allowed them to communicate over distances? Put to flight a pack of ravenous dogs? Locate gold? And hoist him onto a horse? What kind of mind was it that could lift a glider from the ground? With powers like that, the mutants did not need technology.

"We're a new species," Laura went on. "I think we've hardly begun to learn, hardly begun to use our full potential. We don't yet know our own minds, how they work, what they can do."

Alpha and omega, Simon thought savagely.

He was the last of his breed.

She was the first.

And like *Homo sapiens* the mutants would find out they were not perfect.

Laura read his mind.

"No!" she said. "Why won't you listen? Why can't you see? That was your way, not ours! Life is too precious for us to damage or destroy! What's left belongs to all of us. We can share it, Simon, and we don't need to fight or kill."

Simon looked at her in scorn. For all her powers Laura was completely naïve, and those who came from the government bunker would have no scruples. They might be willing to beg for house room among the mutant settlements, but once it was granted, once they were all established, they would begin to take over. No one from the bunker would be willing to accept subservience. It was they who would become masters, and the mutants would be their slaves, put to work planting, and mining, and manufacturing machines. Mutants would build the underground cities, and fulfill their human dreams.

"You'll fight when you have to," Simon assured her. "When it's either us or you, you'll fight."

"Except that there's not many left of you," Laura pointed out. "And every year there are fewer. What is your infant mortality rate? And living among us is it likely to increase? Interbreed too much among yourselves and your genetic strain will weaken. Interbreed with us and you'll father mutant children. It's inevitable, Simon. One way or another your kind is going to die out. Whether we decide to preserve you as a species depends upon your willingness to cooperate with us. The rest of your life is all you can count on, Simon. And you can't make us do anything we don't wish to do. Our minds are stronger than yours, remember?"

"You could control us?" Simon asked sickly.

"Like dogs if we have to," Laura said.

The firelight seemed cold.

And there was nothing more to say.

ooo

Simon sat on an outcrop of rock. Daylight brightened around him, and the valley below was shrouded in mist. He was a shivering, useless lump of human flesh, numb with cold, unable to help himself. His injured leg was stiff and hurting, but pain no longer mattered. Nothing mattered anymore. Laura had stripped away the last vestiges of pride, and defeat had nothing to do with war. It was an emotional experience, a sense of futility as relentless as grief. He had tried to fight it, lashed out in anger against everything Laura was, but all that remained was the final acknowledgment of her supremacy, the final giving up.

His caftan was soaked with overnight dew, but the gray haze held a promise of sun. It did not cheer him any. He could not live in it, not without Laura. He would have to go crawling to her for everything he needed. It was her world now, not his, and he heard her saddling the horse, talking to it softly, making ready to go. She did not know what she had done to him. She did not know she had finally killed his hope.

It might have been easier to bear if the mutants had conquered them, taken them by force and stormed the bunker. In war or enslavement, Simon could have retained a kind of purpose, a concept of eventual freedom. But Laura was not his enemy. He *had* no enemy, except himself.

It was himself he had to accept, not Laura . . . his own humanity . . . his pride, his aggression, his mistaken belief that he was lord over all creation and made in the image of God. There was no proof of that, and there never had been. If God was everywhere, then He was no more in Simon than in the woodlouse that crawled at his feet, in the piebald horse and the seed heads of grasses. And if God was in him, then He was in Laura too, and in that case she was right—the world was made for sharing.

He wanted to squash the woodlouse underfoot, but instead he stared at it. Its segments were pale, almost white, another mutation.

Everything mutated, his mother had said, changed by the sunlight that he was unable to bear. And back in his childhood, Grandfather Harnden had told him the world was once green, but Simon saw it sheened with white . . . filigree hairs on leaves and grassblades forming a natural protection, and a white-eyed bird whistling on a clump of stinging weeds. Laura's world was different from the old one, each species subtly altered, adapting as his kind never had. He found himself wishing that he had been born a mutant.

In a last moment of anger Simon picked up a stone and hurled it over the edge, saw it bounce and strike, go rattling down the tumbled banks of earth and rock, gorse and bracken, toward the unseen water below. He could vaguely make out the ruins of Timberley Abbey, gaunt and gray in a sea of mist. The first rays of sun gilded the opposite hill, turned trees to gold, shining on leaf hairs and dew. He could feel it burning the back of his neck and automatically raised his hood. Strange how he still retained an instinct for survival, self-preservation against all the odds. He clung to his own little life as if something inside him believed, in spite of everything, it was still worth living.

It was, of course. Never mind what his kind had done in the past, or what Laura's kind would do in the future; what mattered to Simon were his own prospects of life. He had no intention of spending the next fifty or so years holed up inside a dark festering bunker, half starved and shivering with cold. Harris had filled his head with electrical principles, solar satellites, and rebuilding the national grid, yet all Simon would inherit in reality was a defunct generator that he did not want. Mutant society might not be the kind of advanced technological society they had dreamed of in the bunker, but it was surely an improvement in living conditions. Simon would have good food, fine clothes, be comfortably housed. What more could he ask?

Nothing, he thought, and government by mutants could be no worse than government by his own kind.

He had to swallow his pride and accept, think of his own future and never mind the future of his kind. It was too late for *Homo sapiens*, but it was not too late for him. It was not too late to make his life a good one, to grow and give and gain in a personal way. He could never live up to Laura mentally or genetically, but he could evolve emotionally and spiritually, and adapt to the mutant way of life. And if he did that, it would not be defeat but victory.

He lifted his head. Below, in the valley, the mist was clearing. He saw a flicker of river water, and the Abbey walls glistened like gold. Roof tiles shone amber in the light. It should have been a ruin, a gothic pile immortalized by poets of the past. But the mist revealed . . . turrets and towers, sunlight reflecting from the window glass, and a town built around it, gold and glittering in the Midas touch of morning, streets and houses of old yellow stone.

Simon caught his breath. He had not known the world before the holocaust, but Grandfather Harnden had told him no tales of a city such as this. Yet he recognized it: El Dorado out of human legends . . . the celestial city become reality. We build cathedrals, Laura had said. And they had also built a city, molten and shimmering beside an English river. It seemed to flow into the land around it, melt with the green-white sheen of wooded hills and water meadows until the whole valley glowed and the glory stunned him.

"Timberley," said Laura. "It was what I wanted to show you. It's always best seen at this time of day."

A few hours ago Simon would have hated her, but hatred had no place in a scene like this. He could understand how she felt about Timberley. It was like a scrap of heaven fallen to earth, the resurrection of something sacred, an architect's triumph, its foundations buried in time. No man could hate what was truly holy.

"It's beautiful," he said simply.

Laura sat beside him on the rock. She too looked beautiful, a golden girl with a sheen on her fur and her pale hair shot with sunlight, like a living fragment of the scene below, perfectly belonging.

"Do you know its history?" she asked.

"It was sacked by Henry the Eighth," he replied.

"A man destroyed it, and a man rebuilt it," she said. "Maybe you know of him? His name was Dwight Allison?"

Simon stared at her.

"Dwight Allison built *that?*"

"He designed it," Laura confirmed. "He saw what it could be, dreamed the street plans and the houses, the stained-glass patterns of the Abbey windows, its columns and arches, its roof vaults and gardens. He dreamed it and we constructed it. He dreamed our settlement, too. But that was long ago, before I was born. Lilith thought you might have heard of him."

"My mother married his brother," Simon said.

"He died," said Laura. "Five years ago."

Dwight had died, but his city lived on.

It was a legacy worth leaving.

"Back in the bunker no one speaks of him," said Simon. "My mother would never tell me what he did, some kind of sabotage, I think. My father said he was a traitor."

"He was an artist and visionary," said Laura. "And we set his visions free. We gave him all he needed, and he gave us Timberley. What visions do you have, Simon? What will you give us in return for all we give you? Will you rebuild the great bridge across the Severn? Will you give us heat and energy and light? Operating techniques for organ transplants? A transport system? What will you give?"

Simon stared at her.

But her gaze stayed fixed on the golden city.

"It needn't even be a concrete thing," she mused. "Ideas are enough. Ideas can become a philosophy and change the world. It wasn't only the nuclear holocaust that made us what we are. It was men like Johnson and women like blind Kate. They taught us to be better people. Taught us to give and share, care about everything and damage nothing. It was your kind who envisioned us, just as Dwight envisioned that city down there. Great people of the past have always dreamed of a future world, and we inherited those dreams. We have the potential to make them reality. Do you understand what I'm saying?"

"I understand," Simon said softly. "But I don't quite see . . ."

"Men like Johnson," said Laura, "and women like blind Kate, founders of settlements—they gave us all they could, but they didn't know everything. They didn't know what you know, Simon. In your government bunkers you have kept alive a knowledge that we need. It would take us generations to sift through all the information collected in books and learn to apply it. By that time we may have lost the ability to understand. Those portions of our brains that are capable of calculative workings out could have fallen into disuse. Psychic powers are very important. Intuitive knowing is very important. But conscious understanding and logical reasoning are equally important. Without knowing how to reason things out, we stand on the brink of a new dark age. That's why we need you, Simon. That's why we're willing to help you stay alive. We need what you know in the bunkers. We need your technological understanding before it's lost forever. Now do you see?"

Simon nodded.

He saw everything, as clear as day.

∘∘∘

Simon did not go on to Timberley. Riding high on Timms' back, with Laura walking beside him, he headed back across the moorland hills of west Gloucestershire. The world had not ended at the Devil's Pulpit. Instead, it had begun. In that golden glittering city and in Laura's words he had seen a future for himself. *Homo sapiens* might be virtually extinct, but all that was worthwhile in them was still going on: great thoughts, great works, great love. Nothing worthwhile was ever wasted. It only evolved and mutated. The vision always survived.

Cool wind fluttered his caftan, and dark glasses protected his eyes from the sun. He wore white linen gloves and a face mask, which the mutants had fashioned for him during the previous afternoon, his skin cocooned from the vicious light. Genetically vulnerable, he would always need protection. But freedom was not necessarily a physical thing. Freedom was a mind released from worry and struggle, released from the impositions of society, free to follow its own inclinations, its own thoughts. And Simon's mind soared, cloud high, escaped at last from the confines of the bunker into a world of unlimited possibilities.

What will you give us? Laura had asked. What visions do you have? A system of solar satellites . . . computerized ground stations . . . a network of power cables . . . and every settlement provided with heat and light? Theoretically it had always been possible. What made it impossible was Simon's inability to manufacture component parts. He could work a computer, but he could not build one. He could not build a launch rocket or extract the necessary fuel for it. In the bunker they had the knowledge, but not the practical wherewithal. He wondered just how much Laura's kind were offering.

"Some of us will need laboratories," he said.

"There's at least one empty workroom in every settlement," Laura informed him. "And if they can't be converted, we can build separate units."

"We'll need specialized equipment too . . . precision tools . . . wiring for electrical circuits . . . silicon chips, copper cables, sheet metal. Where's all that going to come from?"

"We have artisans who can work to your specifications," said Laura.

"And where's your power going to come from? You can't perform laser surgery without power. You can't have a working technology without power. Supposing we could build my solar satellites—supposing we built the reflector shields and launch rockets—would you be able to supply the necessary fuel? Can you extract oil from under the North Sea?"

Laura frowned.

"Fossil fuels are pollutants," she objected.

"We need them to provide the necessary thrust."

"Talk to Tyler," Laura said.

"Psychokinetic impulse? Is that possible?"

"I don't know," said Laura. "I'm not sure Tyler knows either. That's exactly why we need you. We need to know what's possible, and how it's possible. We need you to work it out and then teach us."

Simon pondered, jabbed his foot into Timms' flank. It was a staggering hypothesis, mind blasting into space. If he could calculate the impulse and tonnage lift available from a one-second burst of mental energy, and how long the mutant mind was able to sustain the output, and if one mind could work in unison with others . . . then they might reach the moon again in his lifetime. His imagination raced decades ahead— minds monitoring spaceflight, before coming back to earth. Firstly they needed to calculate the range and accuracy of telepathic thought transference and re-establish an international communications network.

Communications was not Simon's department, but still he was curious. He wondered to what extent mutant minds could be melded together to form a gestalt, if each could become directly aware of what the other knew, thus speeding up the learning process. He wondered if each mind possessed the full range of psychic abilities, to what extent they could be developed, and if their application was learned or inherent. And what about teleportation? Could they transfer matter through space? Transfer themselves as some advanced yogis had once claimed to do? Just how far could mutants transcend the limitations of their physical bodies? What was the principle behind paranormal functioning? How did it work? And why? There were too many questions that as yet had no answers. What Laura was Simon had hardly begun to understand.

"Listen," he said. "About these psychic powers of yours—do they originate solely from inside your mind? I mean . . . do you actually generate them? When you're divining for metal, do you feel energy flowing out of you? How exhausted is Tyler after an hour of flying? Or do you become a channel for some kind of external energy, a cosmic life force? The source of creative spirit? Do you feel any fluctuations in your psychic ability, or can you maintain a constant level? I need to know exactly what we're dealing with."

Simon glanced around when Laura did not answer. Stark on the horizon behind him was the tower of Rushfield church. He had passed it by without even seeing, urged Timms to a trot, and left Laura behind. Now she came running across the grass and heather, her pale hair streaming in the wind, trying to catch up with him. Simon heaved on the reins and waited impatiently. He wanted to reach the settlement, begin work immediately. He had to establish a basic theory before he could begin to apply it. He wanted satellites in orbit . . . the solar panels shifted from Avon . . . a horse and cart. Timms stamped restlessly, sensing his mood, as if he too was eager to get going. Panting for breath, Laura drew level, grasped the bridle, and hung on.

"You're going too fast," she complained.

"We can both get there quicker if we ride together," Simon said.

She looked up at him.

White eyes trying to read his mind.

"I'm a mutant," she reminded him.

"What's wrong with that?" he asked.

"You didn't want me touching you."

"I was stupid then."

Laura stood there, staring up at him, as if she could not believe he had changed so much and needed to be convinced. He held out his hand, inviting her, a mutant girl with white eyes and albino fur, who did not know they were related.

"You're my cousin," he told her.

"We're all cousins to the apes," she said consolingly.

"I don't mean it in an evolutionary sense. This is for real. Blind Kate is my mother's sister."

"Your mother is Amelia Harnden?"

"Ophelia," Simon corrected. "Ophelia Allison now."

"You told blind Kate you'd never heard of her!"

"I lied," Simon admitted.

Laura was angry.

He could feel how angry she was.

And her voice was bitter.

"Why?" she asked. "Why lie to her? What harm would it have done to admit you knew her? Was even that too much for you to give? A little pleasure to an old blind woman? What kind of person are you, Simon?"

Simon bit his lip. He knew what he had been . . . mean, selfish, lying out of pride, unable to accept that he was related. He had thought himself the highest form of life, *Homo sapiens*, the chosen species. It was not easy knowing he was not, harder still to confess the truth of himself.

"I'm human," he said. "I've already told you that. It's the excuse for everything vile our kind has ever done; and it's my excuse too. Blind Kate said I would learn, and I surely have, and I'm not proud of myself. Blind Kate will understand. I'll tell her about my mother when we return to the settlement. And I'm willing to apologize for all the things I've thought about you. Now will you ride with me . . . please?"

She hesitated, a beautiful girl in a white woollen gown, her hair hanging golden in the sunlight. She was as human as he was, sprung from the same stock, nearer to perfection but still unsure of herself. Maybe they had shared the same distaste of each other. Maybe she too was reluctant to grasp the gloved hand of friendship that Simon held out toward her.

"Please?" he repeated softly.

Laura made up her mind, smiled and accepted, and mounted behind him. Slim arms gripped around his waist, tightened as Timms moved on. Thousands of years of strife-ridden history resolved itself in them, the wastage of centuries made good in a moment of time. They had reconciled their human past. Spiritually, mentally, and emotionally, they accepted each other . . . two people on a piebald horse, their voices crying in the wind.

"Is your mother at the settlement?"

"She died when I was born," Laura replied.

"I wish Grandfather Harnden could have seen you."

"Is he dead too?"

"When I was a child. Weird, when you think of it. One man . . . two different progeny, spanning two different worlds. And now we meet."

"I think it's wonderful!" said Laura.

Maybe *she* was wonderful, Simon thought. She saw veils of ultraviolet light shining over a rainbow-colored earth, electrical auras around all living things, and she heard in her mind mutants speaking over the distances. She was not a genetic throwback. She was an evolutionary consequence. For her, millions had died and blind Kate had survived. For her, the world evolved and apes became human. She maintained the continuity of creation and bestowed a meaning upon everything. Grandfather Harnden's seed had flowered, not into Simon, but into her.

Maybe God had planned it this way, dreamed of Laura among the dust of nebulas and stars, had all things move toward her making. And now she would inherit it all, a girl with her arms around him, warm and touching and covered with white fur. She would inherit the standing stones on the high horizon that marked the rise and fall of mankind. She would inherit the earth that had once belonged to them, and reap the knowledge of their minds. Simon stroked her hand. He did not begrudge her. He did not begrudge any of her kind. He would give to them as much as he could, for they were better than he was . . . *Homo superior*, the children of the dust.

F